## "You don't think he's out there, do you?" Katie asked.

Suddenly a light flashed, and the small storage shed that abutted the fence burst into flames.

Shocked, Katie jumped back, instinctively covering her belly as Tony's arms gently wrapped around her to steady her.

"Get your cell phone, go in the bathroom, lock the door and call 911. Don't open the door until I get back." He hooked Rusty to the leash and walked to the door.

She was still standing in the hall, feet planted on the floor.

"Go. I'll be back as soon as I can," Tony said, hand on the doorknob, dark eyes staring into hers.

### TRUE BLUE K-9 UNIT:

These police officers fight for justice
with the help of their brave canine partners.

Aside from her faith and her family, there's not much **Shirlee McCoy** enjoys more than a good book! When she's not hanging out with the people she loves most, she can be found plotting her next Love Inspired Suspense story or trekking through the wilderness, training with a local search-and-rescue team. Shirlee loves to hear from readers. If you have time, drop her a line at shirlee@shirleemccoy.com.

## Books by Shirlee McCoy

### Love Inspired Suspense

#### *True Blue K-9 Unit*

*Sworn to Protect*

#### *FBI: Special Crimes Unit*

*Night Stalker*
*Gone*
*Dangerous Sanctuary*
*Lone Witness*

#### *Mission: Rescue*

*Protective Instincts*
*Her Christmas Guardian*
*Exit Strategy*
*Deadly Christmas Secrets*
*Mystery Child*
*The Christmas Target*
*Mistaken Identity*
*Christmas on the Run*

Visit the Author Profile page at Harlequin.com for more titles.

# SWORN TO PROTECT

## SHIRLEE MCCOY

H HARLEQUIN® LOVE INSPIRED® SUSPENSE

Special thanks and acknowledgment are given to Shirlee McCoy for her contribution to the True Blue K-9 Unit miniseries.

Recycling programs for this product may not exist in your area.

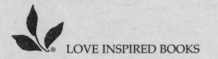

LOVE INSPIRED BOOKS

ISBN-13: 978-1-335-23243-4

Sworn to Protect

www.Harlequin.com

**Printed in U.S.A.**

Whither shall I go from thy spirit? or whither shall I flee from thy presence? If I ascend up into heaven, thou art there: if I make my bed in hell, behold, thou art there. If I take the wings of the morning, and dwell in the uttermost parts of the sea; Even there shall thy hand lead me, and thy right hand shall hold me.

*−Psalm* 139:7-10

To the men and women in our armed forces,
the true heroes of our world.

# ONE

Once upon a time, Katie Jameson could have sprinted up two flights of stairs, raced down a hall and corralled twenty-five fifth graders with ease. She could have finished her workday, gone to the gym, worked out, made dinner and had a smile on her face when her husband returned home. Once upon a time—when Jordan had been alive and Katie had not been nine months pregnant—she had been energetic, enthusiastic and filled with hope.

Now, she was just tired.

Her mother-in-law's constant chatter wasn't making her any less so. Katie loved Ivy. She appreciated how much she and her husband, Alexander, had done since Jordan's death. But, she had not been sleeping well these past few weeks. The pregnancy was nearing its end. She felt huge and unwieldy, her body uncomfortable and unfamiliar.

And, Jordan was gone. Murdered. The reason for it was as shocking as his death had been. Martin Fisher, a man Katie had gone out with twice before she had begun dating Jordan, had become obsessed with her and decided that getting Jordan out of the way would clear a path to the relationship he longed for.

The guilt Katie felt over that was almost overwhelming.

No matter how many people told her that it wasn't her fault, that she couldn't blame herself for Martin's insane bid to win her love, she couldn't help thinking that if she had turned down his invitation when he had asked her out to lunch a few years ago, Jordan would still be alive.

She swallowed down tears, refusing to let her mother-in-law see her sorrow. Ivy had lost her son. That grief had to be almost unbearable. Somehow, though, she had managed to pull herself together and focus on her three remaining sons, her granddaughter and, of course, Katie and the impending baby.

Ivy had done everything she could to make certain Katie didn't feel alone during the pregnancy. If she had not been able to attend obstetric visits with her, Ivy had one of Jordan's brothers go. Someone was always there, sitting in the waiting room.

But, no amount of in-law love could make up for the fact that Jordan was gone. Over seven months now.

She missed him every day.

Today, she missed him even more.

They should have been at home, checking the hospital bag to make sure everything was packed for the big day. They should have been putting the finishing touches on the nursery, putting away baby diapers and bibs, and making certain that their daughter's home would be warm, welcoming and ready.

"Are you okay, dear?" Ivy asked, her voice echoing through the quiet corridor of the medical center. Unlike other obstetric patients, Katie had not been ushered to an exam room. She was being taken to Dr. Ritter's office—a corner room in the far reaches of the medical building. This wasn't a normal appointment. This was an appointment designed to put Katie at ease, to make sure she felt comfortable and confident as she reached her due date.

"Just a little tired," she replied.

"Are you sure? Alex and I both feel that you've been pensive these last few days. More quiet than usual. We don't want to pry, but we also don't want to miss cues that you need more help."

"You've given me plenty of help, and I'm fine. The baby is getting big, and I'm getting uncomfortable. That's all there is to my pensiveness." She kept her voice light and offered a quick smile.

"We thought maybe…"

"What?"

"I hate to even bring it up." Ivy glanced at the nurse who was leading them down the hall, her voice little more than a whisper as she continued. "But, Martin Fisher's escape from the psychiatric hospital has to have put you on edge."

"It has. I'm not going to lie. I feel nervous, but the police and K-9 team are working hard to find him. They aren't going to let him get to me. And, God is still in control." The last one was what she was clinging to. Knowing that God was in charge. That He had a plan.

That no matter what, He would work things out for His good.

"Yes. He is. And, you're right—the NYPD is doing everything in its power to bring Martin in. I just… I don't want you to worry. Not now. Now, with the baby's birth so close."

"I'm trying not to," she said, pasting on another phony smile. She wanted to relax and enjoy the last days and weeks before the baby arrived, but how could she not worry? Martin Fisher was out there somewhere. So far, he had stayed away, but she knew that might not last forever. He might be biding his time, waiting for the right opportunity to come after her. She was the object of his obsession, the reason he had killed Jordan and, maybe, the purpose behind his escape. If he did come after her, there were three possible outcomes.

He could kidnap her and hide her somewhere she'd never be found. In his twisted mind, the baby would be his.

He could kill her—in the classic "if I can't have you, no one can" scenario.

He could try either of the above, and the NYPD would get to him first.

She was counting on the third option. Jordan had been the chief of the NYC K-9 Command Unit. His three brothers were all cops. They were committed to apprehending Martin before he could cause more harm.

She would be safe. Her baby would be safe. Katie had to be believe that.

"Here we are," the nurse said, pushing open a door at the end of the hall. Young, with a bright smile and eyes the color of dark chocolate, she knew why Katie was being seen in the doctor's office rather than an exam room. Everyone who worked at the clinic was aware of the circumstances surrounding the pregnancy—that the baby's father had been murdered, that he had been one of New York's finest.

What they didn't know—what they couldn't—was how loved Jordan had been. How kind. How good of a father he had planned to be.

"Thank you," Katie murmured, blinking back tears. She hated crying in public.

Just like she hated the pity she could see in the nurse's eyes.

"Is there anything I can get you while you're waiting?" the nurse asked.

"I'm good." Katie stepped into the doctor's office, took a seat on one of the leather chairs that faced his desk and dropped her purse on the floor near her feet. She had been in this room before. Just a week after Jordan had died, she had attended her first prenatal appointment. Dr. Ritter had met with her here before taking her to the exam room.

"Okay. You let me know if you change your mind. Dr. Ritter will be with you shortly. He's just delivered a baby, but he'll arrive at the clinic soon. Your next prenatal exam is scheduled for next week, right?"

"Yes."

"Who knows?" The nurse smiled. "Maybe the baby will be here before then."

"Wouldn't that be lovely!" Ivy exclaimed, her cheerfulness a little too bright and a little too brittle. The previous day, she had been talking excitedly about the Thanksgiving meal she was planning. Ivy was the consummate hostess. She loved to cook and entertain, and she had invited a dozen people to join the family for Thanksgiving.

The house would be full.

But, one Jordan-sized space would remain empty.

Ivy was as aware of that as Katie.

The nurse smiled again and departed.

For a moment, the room was silent except for the soft hum of the heat blowing through the floor vents.

Ivy cleared her throat and settled into the chair next to Katie. "It's going to be okay," she said.

"I know," Katie lied.

She didn't know.

No matter how much she wanted to trust God's plan, she couldn't stop worrying that she wouldn't be enough for the child she was carrying. Good enough. Smart enough. Strong enough. Loving enough. *Parent* enough to make up for the fact that the baby didn't have a father.

*This wasn't the plan, God.*

*This wasn't what was supposed to happen.*

*How am I going to do this alone?*

How many times had she prayed those words since Jordan had died?

Too many.

And, there was never any answer. Never any clear direction as to how she could be all of the things the baby would need.

"You don't look like you know it," Ivy replied. She had aged since Jordan's death; lines that had not been there before bracketed her mouth and fanned out from her eyes. She was a beautiful woman. Strong. Determined. But, losing her son had cost her.

"Like I said, I'm tired. It's hard to sleep with this one kicking me in the ribs all night." She patted her belly. No fake smile this time. She was too tired to try.

"I remember those days," Ivy said with a soft smile. "Jordan was especially prone to keeping me up. It's not surprising that his child is the same." She reached out and laid her hand on the swell of Katie's abdomen.

When she pulled away, there were tears in her eyes. "He would have loved this."

"Yes, he would have."

"And, he would have been a great father. He was always so good with children."

"The kids at school loved him," Katie agreed.

Jordan had been born and raised in Queens, and he had had a passion for mentoring the youth there. He had often visited schools with his K-9 partner, Snapper. He had also taught self-defense classes at the local YMCA. He had been Katie's instructor when she had moved to New York and taken a self-defense class. Just in case.

A year later, he had visited the school where she was teaching. They'd bumped into each other in the hall. The rest had happened fast. Long conversations. Walks in the park. Jokes. Laughter.

Love.

Marriage.

They should have had their happily-ever-after.

Instead, Katie was alone. Getting ready to give birth to their baby.

"I wish I'd asked the nurse to bring me something to drink," she murmured, her throat tight with emotion.

"They have water in the waiting room. And, coffee. Would you like me to bring you something?" Ivy offered.

"Would you mind? I'd love a cup of water."

"Of course, I don't mind. Should you stay here alone, though? The boys would have my head if they thought I'd left you unattended even for a minute."

"I'll be fine, Ivy," Katie assured her. "Don't worry. You'll be back in five seconds."

Ivy looked unsure, but then stood and hurried from the room.

Just as Katie had hoped she would. She didn't want to talk about Jordan. Not now. Not when she felt exhausted and emotional. She wanted to keep focused on the birthing plan, on staying safe, on making sure she did what her brothers-in-law and the police asked her to. Since Martin's escape, the Jameson brothers had been escorting her almost everywhere. Today, though, they were attending a training seminar in Manhattan. They'd asked fellow K-9 officer Tony Knight to run patrols past the medical clinic. They'd told her to be careful and aware. To stay close to their mother. To listen to her gut.

Right now, her gut was saying she was exhausted. That she needed to sleep. That she didn't want to think about the danger or the tragedy.

Someone knocked on the door.

"Come in," she called, bracing herself for the meeting with Dr. Ritter.

The door swung open and a man in a white lab coat stepped in, holding her chart close to his face.

Only, he was not the doctor she was expecting.

Dr. Ritter was in his early sixties with salt-and-pepper hair and enough extra weight to fill out his lab coat. The doctor who was moving toward her had dark hair and a muscular build. His scuffed shoes and baggy lab coat made her wonder if he were a resident at the hospital where she would be giving birth.

"Good morning," she said, feeling unsettled. She had been meeting with Dr. Ritter since the beginning of the pregnancy. He understood her feelings about the birth. He probably suspected a lot of the fear and trepidation she tried to hide. She never had to say much at her appointments, and that was the way she liked it. Talking about the fact that Jordan wouldn't be around for his daughter's birth, her childhood, her life always brought Katie close to the tears she despised.

"Morning," he mumbled.

She could see his forehead and his brows but not much else. That seemed strange. Usually, doctors looked up from the charts when they entered the exam rooms.

"Is Dr. Ritter running late?" she asked, uneasiness joining the unsettled feeling in the pit of her stomach.

"He won't be able to make it," the man said, lowering the charts and grinning.

She went cold with terror.

She knew the hazel eyes, the lopsided grin, the high forehead. "Martin," she stammered, jumping to her feet.

"Sorry it took me so long to get to you, sweetheart.

I had to watch from a distance until I was certain we could be alone."

"Watch?" she repeated.

"They wanted to keep me in the hospital, but our love is too strong to be denied. I escaped for you. For us. And, I've been so close to you these past few weeks. It's been torture." He lifted a hand, and if she had not jerked back, his fingers would have brushed her cheek.

He scowled. "Have they brainwashed you? Have they turned you against me?"

"You did that yourself when you murdered my husband," she responded and regretted it immediately.

He grabbed her arm and dragged her the few feet to his side. "We're leaving here, Katie. We're going to a quiet place where we can be together."

"I'm not going anywhere with you," she replied, trying to yank her arm away, but his grip was firm, his fingers digging through the soft knit fabric of her sweater.

"Katie? I brought juice and water." Ivy appeared in the doorway, a paper cup in each hand.

Her eyes widened as she saw Martin, her gaze dropping to his hand, then jumping to Katie's face. "What's going on?"

"Nothing you need to worry about," Martin responded, pulling a gun from beneath the lab coat.

The cups dropped from Ivy's hands, water and juice spilling onto the tile floor, her screams spilling into the hall.

"Shut up!" Martin screamed, yanking Katie forward as he slammed the butt of the gun into the side of Ivy's head. She went down hard, her body limp, eyes closed.

Katie clawed at Martin's hand, trying to free herself and get to her mother-in-law. She had taken self-defense classes. She should know how to do this, but panic and pregnancy made her movements clumsy and slow.

"Stop!" he said. One word. Uttered with cold deliberation. The barrel was suddenly pressed into her stomach. She could feel the baby wiggling and turning.

She froze.

Just like he had commanded. Everything in her focused on keeping the baby alive.

"That's better. You wouldn't want the baby to get hurt in the scuffle," he growled, yanking her away from the office. Several nurses were racing toward them, one of them yelling into a cell phone. A doctor barreled around the corner, eyes wide with shock as she saw what the commotion was about.

"Everyone just stay cool," Martin said, the gun still pressed into Katie's abdomen. "I'm not here to hurt anyone. I'm just here for my wife."

She stiffened at the word but was too afraid to argue.

"I've called the police," the nurse with the cell phone said. "They'll be here any minute."

"Good for them," Martin responded. "Everyone get out of our way." He pushed open the stairwell door and dragged Katie down two flights of steps. She was stumbling, trying to keep her feet under her, terrified that she'd fall and hurt the baby, that the gun would go off, that he'd get her outside and take her wherever he intended.

"Stop." She gasped, panicking as they rushed into

the lobby on the lower level of the building. "I can't breathe."

"You're breathing just fine, my love," he murmured, smiling tenderly into her face as he pressed the gun more deeply into her stomach.

"Martin, really. I can't."

There were people all around, shocked, afraid. Watching but not intervening, and she couldn't blame them. Martin was armed and obviously dangerous, his eyes gleaming with the fire of his delusions.

"Hey! You! Let her go!" A security guard raced toward them. No gun. Nothing but a radio and a desire to help.

Martin moved the gun, and Katie had seconds to shove him sideways, to try to ruin his aim, save the guard and free herself.

The bullet slammed into the wall, and a woman shrieked.

For a split second, Katie was free, running back to the stairwell, clawing at the doorknob, trying to get back up the stairs and away from Martin.

He grabbed her jacket and dragged her backward, nearly unbalancing her. She felt the barrel of the gun against the side of her neck.

"Don't make me hurt you, Katie," he whispered, his lips brushing her ear.

She froze again.

"That's my girl. Now, let's go." He grabbed her hand, the gun slipping away from her neck, and dragged her outside.

* * *

Tony Knight had been a police officer for enough years to know how to stay calm in the most challenging of circumstances.

The current situation demanded every bit of the discipline he had learned during his years on the force.

He watched as Martin Fisher dragged Katie across the crowded parking lot. She wasn't fighting or protesting, and Tony couldn't blame her. Martin was swinging the firearm in the direction of anyone who dared to call for him to stop.

Katie had to be terrified.

Katie.

His best friend's *widow*.

The word still made his chest tight and his jaw clench. Jordan should be alive, getting ready to celebrate the birth of his first child.

Martin Fisher was responsible for his death.

That was reason enough to take him down.

But, Tony came from a long line of police officers. He believed in the criminal justice system. He believed in due process and trial by jury. He did not believe in vigilantism. To get Katie safely away from Martin, Tony would use whatever force was required. But, he also didn't believe in risking the lives of innocent civilians—Katie and the big crowd watching. The moment Tony pulled the trigger, so would Martin—with the gun pointed at Katie's heart.

Tony also didn't like the idea of firing his weapon when he was aiming at a target so close to Katie.

"Let her go, Martin," he called, his service weapon aimed at the killer's head, his police dog, Rusty, by his side. The chocolate-colored Lab growled quietly.

Trained in search and rescue, he had a powerful build and split-second reaction time. If asked to, he'd go after the perp and attempt to take him down.

Tony didn't want to ask him to. Martin would shoot Rusty and have the gun aimed back at Katie in a heartbeat.

"Or what?" Martin asked, his yellow-green eyes focused on Tony.

"I don't think you want to find out," Tony responded, trying to keep him talking and buy some time. Backup was on the way. A 911 call had been placed moments before he had arrived at the medical center. He had been running his regular patrol route through Queens, detouring past the four-story brick building every few minutes. Worried, because he knew that none of Jordan's brothers had been available to accompany Katie to her appointment.

"You're a big talker, Knight," Martin snapped, yanking Katie backward. Of course, he knew Tony's name. He was obsessed with everyone and everything that had anything to do with Katie's life.

"I'm also big on action. Let her go."

Martin scowled. He was moving Katie to the edge of the paved lot. A few feet of lush grass separated the medical clinic's property from the edge of Forest Park. Tall oak trees marked the eastern edge of the public area.

"But, you won't risk Katie's or the baby's life," Martin said. "For the sake of your buddy Jordan, if nothing else."

He was right.

Tony couldn't take a chance. He was confident in his ability to hit his mark, but if Katie moved, if Martin yanked her at just the wrong moment, she or the baby could be injured.

Or, worse.

He couldn't allow that to happen.

"Put your gun down, Martin. Let her go. We'll get you the help you need."

"I don't need help. I need my family." He pulled Katie into his chest, pressing the gun against her side. The barrel was hidden by the soft swell of her abdomen, but Tony could see her face, her blue eyes and her blond ponytail snaking over her shoulder.

"Please, Martin," she said, her voice shaking. "Just let me go. We can talk things out after you've gotten treatment."

"Treatment for what?" Martin asked coldly, his eyes blazing hot in his impassive face.

He was delusional and dangerous, and he was stepping into the grass, dragging Katie with him.

Tony needed to stop him before he made it into the park.

"You were in the hospital," Tony pointed out, stepping closer, his gun dropping to his side. He wanted Martin to be off guard and vulnerable, unprepared for what was going to happen. "And, from what I heard, you were doing well there."

He hadn't actually heard much, but Martin would do just fine locked up in a mental health facility for the remainder of his life.

"I didn't ask for your opinion. Or, the opinion of anyone else," Martin snapped, but the gun had fallen away from Katie's side, and he was glancing back, eyeing the sparse growth of oaks that heralded the beginning of parkland.

The proximity of Forest Park might make it more difficult to apprehend Martin. Tony was determined to get Katie away from the guy, but if Martin managed to disappear into the park, there would be plenty of footpaths and several roads that he could use to make a quick escape.

"Get back in your car," Martin said coldly. "I would never hurt Katie, but Jordan's kid means nothing to me." He jabbed the gun into Katie's stomach, and she winced.

"You can't hurt the baby without hurting the mother," Tony reminded him.

"I'm not as stupid as people think I am. I know a lot of tricks." Martin moved backward, away from Tony, his K-9 vehicle and the parking lot.

Tony unhooked Rusty's lead from his collar so he could release him. Normally the chocolate Lab wouldn't attack. He was a placid, easygoing house companion and a die-hard worker when it came to search and rescue, but he hadn't been trained to unarm dangerous criminals. He did, however, have a fierce desire to protect his pack.

Right now, he was barking, sensing the tension and anxiety and ready to do what he had to in order to make certain his people were safe.

"And don't even think about releasing that dog!"

Martin screamed, the gun shifting away from Katie as he focused on Rusty.

Katie slammed her elbow into his stomach.

Martin gasped and dropped the gun from his hand.

"Go!" Tony shouted, releasing Rusty as Katie darted away.

# TWO

*Fight. Free yourself. Run.*

Jordan's words echoed through Katie's head as she sprinted away. He had said them dozens of times when he had taught the self-defense class she had signed up for a few weeks after taking the job teaching in Queens. The neighborhood had been safe, but she had grown up in the suburbs, and the hustle and bustle of the city had been disconcerting.

Plus, she had been a young woman, alone.

She had wanted to know that she could defend herself.

She had not been thinking about defending an unborn child.

She hadn't been thinking about being a wife or a mother. She had been thinking about living life on her terms. That was something she had not been able to do when she had been a teenager moving through the foster-care system.

Rusty growled and snapped as he dashed by.

She ran in the opposite direction, darting off the

curb, her ankle twisting. She tried to right herself, but the pregnancy made her ungainly, her body front-heavy and cumbersome.

She tripped and went down, hands and knees skidding across asphalt. Someone grabbed her arm and pulled her to her feet. It had to be Martin!

She fought the way Jordan had taught her.

Elbow to the stomach, pushing back into his weight.

"Katie, stop. It's me," Tony said.

She knew his voice.

If she had not been so panicked, she'd have known his gentle touch—his fingers curving lightly around her upper arm.

He had done the same at the funeral, standing beside her as Jordan's coffin was lowered into the ground.

*Ashes to ashes. Dust to dust.*

She stopped struggling and whirled toward the park. "Where did he go?"

There was no sign of Martin, but Rusty was nearing a copse of trees, still barking ferociously. He was trained in search and rescue and had no business going after a deranged and dangerous man.

"Rusty is going to get hurt," she said, her voice shaking. "You need to call him back."

"He'll be okay," Tony responded. He was tracking the dog's movements as he relayed information into the radio.

If he was worried, she couldn't hear it in his voice.

But, then, he was one of New York's finest. Just like Jordan had been. He had great training, a good head on his shoulders and the ability to stay calm even in the most challenging circumstances.

He and Jordan had been best friends.

*My fourth brother.*

How many times had Jordan said that?

And how often had Katie set an extra plate at the dinner table? How often had she watched as the two men tossed balls for their K-9 partners in the yard behind the three-family house they'd shared with the Jameson clan? Countless times. She and Jordan had lived on the second level of the home. His parents just below them. His brothers and young niece above. They were the family she had longed for after her parents had died. They were the connection she had prayed she would have during the years she had spent drifting from one foster home to the next.

She had thought life would keep going in the same positive direction. She had thought—wrongly so—that the tragedy of losing her parents in a car accident when she was ten was enough for a lifetime.

She should have known better.

There was nothing in the Bible about life being easy.

There were no promises made to the faithful.

Except that God would be there. Guiding. Helping. Creating good out of bad.

The problem was Katie couldn't see how anything good could come of losing Jordan. Or, of being stalked by a deranged man.

She shuddered, then her eyes widened. "Ivy! My mother-in-law. He hit her with the gun. Is she all right? I need to know that Ivy is all right!"

Word came over the radio just then that the building was secure, the suspect was on the loose and one victim, Ivy Jameson, had come to and was being treated for a minor head injury.

"Thank God," Katie said, the breath whooshing out of her.

"It's going to be okay," Tony murmured, his hand still on her arm. "We'll get him."

"I hope so," she replied.

His gaze dropped from her face to her belly.

There was a smudge of dirt on her shirt.

"Are you hurt?" he asked, meeting her gaze again.

He had the darkest eyes she had ever seen. Nearly black, the irises all but melding with his pupils.

"I don't think so," she responded. The baby was turning cartwheels, little elbows and feet and hands jabbing and poking. She would be an active child, and Katie wondered if Jordan had been that way.

It bothered her that she didn't know.

They'd known each other for only a few years. They'd met, dated and married so quickly, people had probably wondered at their rush.

"You aren't sure?" Tony released her arm and turned her hands over, frowning as he eyed the scraped and bleeding flesh.

"I'm fine. I just... I'd be better if you were going after Martin. I want him caught."

"We all do," he replied. "I called in the direction Martin took. Police are all over Forest Park, looking for him." He held her gaze for a moment, then motioned at a small group of medical personnel that had emerged from the building and were standing near the clinic's door.

"We need some help over here," he said.

A nurse rushed over.

That was no surprise.

Tony had a way of getting people to do what he wanted. He wasn't manipulative. He wasn't demanding. He simply had an air of confidence that people responded to.

"Mrs. Jameson!" the nurse cried. "I'm so glad you're safe!"

"Me, too," she murmured, suddenly faint, her heart galloping frantically. She couldn't catch her breath, and she sat on the curb, the edges of her vision dark, sounds muted by the frantic rush of blood in her ears.

"Katie?" Tony said, his voice faint, his palm pressed to her cheek. She realized he was crouching in front of her, his face filled with concern. The nurse was beside her, checking the pulse in her wrist.

"I'm okay. I just want Martin caught."

"Me, too." He glanced toward the parking lot's entrance. Several patrol cars were pulling in, with their lights and sirens on.

"You can go, if you want," she said. "There are dozens of people around. Martin would never try to…"

She stopped, because she knew he would try anything to get to her. There was no telling what he might do. No one had imagined that he'd enter the clinic and go after her there, but he had. He had killed Jordan. He'd kill again to get what he wanted.

And, what he wanted was Katie.

Her pulse jumped at the thought, and her abdomen cramped with such surprising intensity, she gasped.

"Hun, are you okay?" the nurse asked, laying a hand on Katie's stomach as if she knew exactly what was happening.

"Yes," she replied, but she wasn't certain.

"Feels like you're having a contraction," the nurse said.

"A contraction?" Tony frowned. "As in the baby is coming?"

"No. We're a couple weeks out from that," Katie managed to say.

The nurse smiled kindly. "The baby will come when he or she decides it's time. If today is the day, there's not a whole lot you can do about it."

"Today can't be the day," Katie said.

"If it is, you'll be fine and so will the baby. You're at what? Thirty-six weeks? That's early, but we deliver thirty-six-weekers all the time. They do remarkably well." The nurse straightened and turned back toward the building. "I'll get a wheelchair, and we'll bring you back into the clinic, hook you up to a fetal monitor and see what's going on."

"Today can't be the day," Katie repeated, but the nurse was already hurrying away.

"She's right," Tony said quietly. "You and the baby will be okay. Even if she arrives today."

"I don't want to give birth until after Martin is caught."

She didn't want to give birth alone, either, but she

didn't tell him that. She hadn't told anyone how afraid she was to go through this without Jordan.

"Like the nurse said, the baby will decide." He smiled gently. "Noah just arrived. I'm going after Martin."

He touched her cheek, then stood.

When he moved away, she could see her brother-in-law, the new chief of the K-9 Command Unit, rushing across the parking lot, his rottweiler partner, Scotty, bounding beside him.

"Katie!" Noah shouted, his expression and voice only hinting at the fear she knew he must be feeling. The baby she was carrying was the Jameson family's last link to Jordan. She knew Jordan's parents and three brothers cared about her, but the baby was blood.

"I'm okay," she assured Jordan's brother. "And so is your mother."

She wasn't sure if he heard.

The police sirens were loud. An ambulance was screaming into the parking lot. A large crowd had formed, the murmur of panicked voices drifting beneath the cacophony of emergency sirens and squawk of radio communications.

There were dozens of people around.

But, somehow, Katie felt completely alone.

Katie and the baby would be fine, Tony told himself as he jogged along the railroad tracks that cut through Forest Park. Rusty was in front of him, following a scent trail through oak leaves that partially covered the railroad ties that stretched between the rails. The Lab had an exceptional nose. They'd spent countless hours

together training in wilderness-air scent and urban re-
covery. They were a team, partners in a way people
who have never been dog handlers couldn't understand.

Jordan had understood. Just like he had understood
the desire to go into law enforcement, the deep-seated
need to see justice done. They had been best friends for
years. Jordan's death had been a blow that Tony was
still trying to recover from.

Martin Fisher was a cold-blooded killer—evil. When
Tony thought about the horrific lengths Martin had gone
to… Threatening to kill Katie via a bomb he'd said he'd
rigged, Martin had forced Jordan to write his own suicide note, then had given him drugs to simulate a heart
attack. The "suicide" had seemed plausible to some, but
not to the Jameson clan or to Tony.

Jordan had been happily married, excited about life
and enthusiastic about the future. He'd had everything
to live for.

The discovery that Jordan had been murdered had not
surprised Tony. He *had* been taken by surprise by the
reason for his best friend's murder. Every police officer
understood the dangers of the job. Tony and Jordan had
discussed what would happen if one of them were killed
in the line of duty. Jordan had promised to always be
there for Tony's family; Tony had, of course, promised
to always be there for Jordan's. During Jordan and Katie's wedding reception, Jordan had pulled Tony aside
and reminded him of that promise.

*If anything happens to me, you'll make sure she's
okay, right?*

*You know I will, but nothing is going to happen to you, bro.*

Something had happened, but not in the way either of them had imagined. There had been no gunfire during a robbery, no ambush during a response to a domestic incident. As far as Tony could ascertain, Jordan hadn't even had a chance to fight. He had been murdered by a man who was obsessed with Katie, and he'd seemed to have been taken as much by surprise as the rest of the team had been.

Jordan's German shepherd partner, Snapper, had been missing since the day the suicide note had been found. Recently the team had learned that Snapper had been picked up by an animal shelter not too long ago and adopted out. The once-majestic canine had been a stray on the streets for so long that he had become unrecognizable. The NYC K-9 Command Unit was attempting to contact the man who had adopted Snapper. So far, they'd had no success.

Jordan would want Snapper home.

He would want Martin prosecuted and tossed in jail.

He wouldn't want anyone on the K-9 unit to circumvent justice and mete out punishment without due process.

Tony knew that. He had been working hard to keep his emotions in check and not allow anger to skew his perspective, but he *was* angry. Jordan had been one of the best. Not just at his police work but at his friendships and his life. He had been loyal, brave and devoted. He should have had decades of service left to the community. He should have grown old with Katie, raised a bunch of kids with her and retired into a life of leisure.

Tony frowned, stepping over a downed tree that had fallen next to the tracks.

He had grown up in Queens and still lived there, renting a one-bedroom floor unit in a multifamily house right on the edge of Forest Hills. He and Rusty spent their downtime in this park, walking the trails and hiking through the oak woods. They both knew the area, and Rusty was confident as he loped ahead. After Tony had freed Rusty from his lead, the dog had circled back to find Tony in the park and then led him here. Like any well-trained search dog, he knew his job. Find the subject and return to the handler again and again, until the handler and the subject were in the same place.

With backup arriving and fanning out across the five-hundred-acre expanse of trees and trails, it wouldn't take long to find Martin if he had stayed in the park. Based on the direction Rusty was heading, Tony didn't think he had. There was a crossroad ahead, dirt and gravel that cut through the park. Vehicles were prohibited, but that didn't keep teens and young adults from driving through.

Rusty sniffed an area in the center of the road, circled around and headed east. Tony followed. Tire tread marks were clearly visible, all of them sprinkled with leaves and debris. They had been there awhile. From the look of things, Martin wasn't in a vehicle.

"Find!" Tony called, encouraging the Lab to keep searching.

Rusty made another circle, sniffing the ground and then raising his head. He had caught the scent again. Tony followed him off the road and into the woods.

The day had the crisp edge of winter, the bright sunlight filtering through a thin tree canopy. From his position, Tony could see a trail that wound its way through the trees.

If Martin knew the area and the park, he would know that the trail led to a busy road and an easy escape. Tony had every reason to believe Martin was familiar with the area. He had been renting an apartment just a few miles away before his arrest for Jordan's murder.

A murder Martin had tried to make look like a suicide. Tony shook his head, unable to stop thinking about it, what Martin had done. *Tried* to do. If he had gotten away with it, Jordan's family would have spent a lifetime trying to understand how they had missed signs of Jordan's depression. They would have wasted energy on unfounded regrets.

The thought still filled Tony with fury.

Again, he had known immediately that Jordan would not have taken his own life. His friend had had too much respect and appreciation for all that God had given him.

There were others who had doubted, though. People who had whispered that Jordan might have had secrets or addictions or relationship troubles that had sent him into a spiraling depression.

Those whispered rumors had only compounded the tragedy of Jordan's death.

Somewhere in the distance a dog barked, the sound carrying on the breeze. Another joined the chorus, the wild baying of a hound on the scent. This was Tony's music, his symphony. He loved the sound of working dogs doing their thing. He loved being part of the NYC K-9 Command Unit. His father had wanted him to follow in his footsteps and become a homicide detective, but Tony enjoyed pounding the pavement, interacting on a daily basis with the community he served. The fact that his job choice had led him into K-9 work was something Tony was constantly grateful for.

He loved what he did.

He loved the life he led.

But, a piece of his soul seemed to have disappeared the day Jordan died.

They had been as close as brothers.

Losing him had left a giant hole in Tony's life.

He had been trying to fill it with work, but even that had begun to feel hollow. There had to be more than long days stretching into long nights and a quiet apartment.

He frowned.

He hadn't been sleeping well lately. That had to be the reason for his melancholy mood. Nearly eight months after Jordan's death, and he was still burning the candle at both ends. In the first few months, he had been trying to figure out exactly what had happened to his friend.

Now, he was desperately trying to get a step ahead of Martin.

He was close. Tony could feel it.

Rusty growled softly, and the warning made the hair on the back of Tony's neck stand on end. He knew his canine partner better than he knew the park or Queens or New York City. Rusty only growled when he sensed danger.

Tony whistled to call the dog back, then stood still,

listening to the sudden silence of the park. A bird took flight, zipping away from a tree a dozen yards away. Leaves rustled. Branches snapped. Someone was coming, and he wasn't being quiet about it.

Tony pulled out his gun and aimed it in the direction of the sound. Martin had dropped his gun near the clinic, but if he'd been able to get his hands on one firearm, he could certainly have another.

Seconds later, a teenager stumbled from the woods, his face ashen. Thin and gangly, his entire body trembling, he looked to be thirteen or fourteen. Probably a kid playing hooky from school who had run into a lot more trouble than he had expected.

"Hold it! Hands where I can see them," Tony shouted.

The kid whirled in his direction, his eyes wide with fear. "Some guy has got my friend. He has a knife to his throat."

Tony didn't need to ask who. He knew. This was exactly what a coward like Martin would do. Find an innocent bystander and use him as a shield during his escape.

"Which way did they go?" Tony asked.

"That way!" The boy pointed through the trees.

"Stay here. Rusty, find!" The Lab plunged into the undergrowth. Tony followed, branches snagging his clothes. Rusty bounded ahead, ears flapping, tail high. He knew where he was going, and he shot straight as an arrow toward the scent pool.

He disappeared into a thicket.

Tony raced after him, radioing in his location and hoping backup would arrive quickly. Martin had already committed murder; there was no reason to believe he wouldn't do it again. The teenager he'd kidnapped could be as easily disposed of as he had been abducted.

Rusty barked, and the sound reverberated throughout the woods.

"Call your dog off!" a man shouted, the voice high-pitched and filled with anger and fear.

Tony plunged into the thicket, pushed through the heavy bramble and thick vines and shoved his way into a small clearing.

Martin was just ahead, his arm around a young teen's waist, a knife held against the boy's throat. Rusty was snapping and growling nearby.

"Let the kid go, Martin," Tony said calmly.

"Call off your dog," Martin responded, the knife nicking flesh, a tiny bead of blood sliding down the kid's throat.

He didn't flinch, didn't cry out. He just stared into Tony's eyes, silently begging for help.

"Rusty, off," Tony commanded.

The Lab continued to growl as he backed off and took his place next to Tony.

"That's better," Martin muttered, stepping backward, the knife blade still pressed against the boy's neck. "Now, put your weapon down, and we'll all be just fine."

"You know I'm not going to do that, Martin."

"Then, I guess this kid is going to die. Just like your buddy." Martin's eyes were cold, his tone emotionless.

"Put the knife down, let the boy go and we'll get you the help you need."

"I don't need help. I need to get back what your friend took from me." Martin nearly spat the words, his gaze suddenly sharp with rage.

"Please let me go," the teen gasped, his eyes wide with fear, the thin trickle of blood staining the collar of his jacket.

"Once we're out of the park and away from the police, you can go on with your day. *If* you cooperate." Martin dragged the boy to the edge of the clearing, his focus on Tony. "None of this needed to happen. *None of it.* Jordan could have had any woman. He didn't have to go after mine."

"Katie was never yours, Martin. You know that." Tony followed Martin across the clearing, Rusty close to his side.

"She was always mine. She will always be mine. She knows that. I know it. It is just the rest of the world that needs to understand." Martin's knife hand slipped away from the boy's neck.

Tony lunged toward Martin, grabbed his wrist and dragged it away from the boy's throat. The teen twisted free, shoving into Tony as he tried to run. He tripped, sprawling on the ground, his shoulders knocking Tony's arm. Tony's hand slipped, and the knife slid across his shoulder, slicing through fabric and flesh. There was no pain. Just the desperate need to regain control of the weapon.

Martin jerked back, the knife still in his hand. He swung, the blade arching through the air inches from Tony's face.

"Back off!" Martin spat as he raised the knife again.

This time Tony was ready.

He gave Martin a two-armed shove backward, pulled out his firearm and aimed for Martin's arm. He didn't want to kill the man. He just needed to stop him. "Freeze!" he yelled, as the teen jumped to his feet and darted between them.

It was the second of opportunity Martin needed.

The knife blade dropped again, this time slicing across the boy's cheek. He darted away, pushing through a patch of brambles and darting from the line of Tony's gunfire.

Blood spurted from the wound in the teen's cheek. He wobbled as Tony shoved past, ready to follow Martin.

"Stay here!" he shouted at the boy.

But, the kid didn't seem interested in listening.

He followed Tony, rushing after him as he shoved through the patch of brambles and called in his location.

"I said, stay put!" Tony repeated, concerned for the boy, but more concerned that Martin would escape again. He had proven to be cunning and dangerous, and he needed to be apprehended before he hurt someone else.

"I'm not staying there waiting for him to come back for me," the teen responded, his voice muffled and faint. One minute he was running behind Tony. The next, he was falling, his scrawny body knocking into Tony as he went down.

"You okay?" Tony asked, still moving. When the teen didn't respond, he glanced back. The kid was lying prone, blood seeping from his cheek, eyes closed. He was clearly unconscious.

Tony itched to go after Martin, but he couldn't leave an injured and unconscious teenager lying in the park alone.

Frustrated, he jogged back, crouching near the young man and feeling for a pulse. Every second he spent there was a second more of distance Martin put between them, but this wouldn't be the end of the chase. As soon as backup arrived, Tony and Rusty would return to the hunt.

*I'll get you*, Tony vowed. For Katie. For Jordan. For himself.

# THREE

Katie didn't like hospitals. The scents and sounds brought back memories she'd rather forget. She had been ten when her parents died. An only child being raised by only children, she had had an idyllic childhood—a pretty house in the suburbs, nice clothes, good food and parents who'd loved her.

That had changed the night of her parents' fifteenth wedding anniversary. She had been at home with a babysitter when a drunk driver had blown through a red light and hit her parents' sedan. Her father had been killed instantly. Her mother had lived for nearly a week. Katie had visited her every day, standing alone in the ICU and listening to the *whoosh* and *beep* of the machines keeping her mother alive. She'd had no grandparents, uncles or aunts to support her as she grieved. Just strangers who had meant well but who had not been able to give her the only thing she had wanted—her parents.

Even now, all these years later, hospitals made her stomach churn.

She touched her abdomen, her fingers skimming across the fetal monitor that was strapped there. The baby was moving, her rapid heartbeat filling the silence of the room. The contractions had ended as abruptly as they'd begun, and for the past two hours, she had been lying in the hospital bed, watching the clock, wondering how Ivy was doing and if Tony and Rusty were all right. Worrying about what Martin might be doing.

He'd tracked her here earlier. Walked right into the clinic, donned a lab coat and fooled everyone he'd passed. He could do it again. Had he managed to circle back to the building? Was he inside right now?

*Breathe*, she told herself. *An officer is stationed outside your room. Martin can't get you. Or, hurt the baby.*

She wanted the thought to be comforting, but Jordan had been tough, strong and smart. Somehow Martin had managed to get to him. If that could happen, anything seemed possible.

She had not heard anything from her father- or brothers-in-law since she had insisted they stay by Ivy's side. They had left reluctantly, but they *had* left. Katie hadn't expected or wanted anything else.

That didn't mean she liked being alone.

For the first hour, regular contractions had distracted her.

Now, with the pain gone, her mind was spinning, her thoughts jumping from one thing to the next. She had spent nearly nine months preparing to give birth without Jordan, but the threat of an early labor, even just by a couple of weeks, had made her realize how desperately she still wanted him there.

He'd promised her a lot of things before they had married.

He had promised her even more when they'd stood in front of friends and family and spoken their vows. He had said he would love her always, that she would be first in his life after God, that he would put her needs in front of his own and be the family she longed for. That he would always be there for her.

She had believed him. But, even in the first few months of their marriage, she had known that her needs were secondary to the needs of the K-9 unit and the community. Jordan had taken his responsibilities to both seriously. He had worked long hours and devoted himself to justice. She had admired that more than she had resented it, but there *had* been a tiny bit of jealousy—a small part of herself that had wondered how they would both feel in a decade or two, after his job had pulled him away from anniversaries and holidays and birthdays a few too many times.

She frowned, shoved aside the blanket that covered her legs and got to her feet. She unhooked the monitor and set it on a table near the bed.

Lately, she had spent too much time looking at the past through a microscopic lens. As if, somehow, that could change all of the things that had happened.

But, of course, no amount of dwelling on her decisions, on the things she had believed and expected, could change the fact that Jordan was dead, that she was alone, that a man who had seemed as innocuous as a buttercup in a field of daisies had killed her husband and nearly kidnapped her.

Martin was deranged.

A dangerous man with a twisted obsession.

And, she was the target of that obsession.

She was the reason Jordan had been murdered.

No matter how much she wanted to, she couldn't forget that, and she couldn't forgive herself.

If she could go back to the days before she and Jordan had met, she would. Instead of being open to all of the new people in her life, she would have ignored Martin when she saw him at the church they had both attended. She wouldn't have chatted with him when they ran into each other in the parking lot after service. She certainly wouldn't have accepted his invitation to coffee the following Sunday morning. Nor would she have had lunch with him the week after that.

To Katie, those had not been real dates. They had been opportunities to get to know a nice guy in her new church community. Martin had been charming. He had also been a Sunday school teacher, a deacon, a man who quoted Scripture and lived a seemingly upright life. Katie hadn't seen any harm in saying yes to his invitations.

If she could go back, she would have known the truth about what lurked beneath Martin's charming exterior. She wouldn't have spoken to him. She wouldn't have gone out with him. She wouldn't have unwittingly sparked the obsession that had cost Jordan his life.

She swallowed a hard lump of grief.

Her clothes were folded neatly and set on a chair near the door. Her purse had been retrieved from Dr. Ritter's office and was sitting on top of them. She grabbed the purse and her clothes and ducked into the bathroom to dress. She wanted to be quick, but pregnancy made her once-athletic body cumbersome and clumsy. By the time she managed to get out of the hospital gown and back into her clothes, a nurse was knocking on the bathroom door.

"Katie? Is everything okay?"

"Fine." She opened the door and smiled as she sidled past the nurse and slid her feet into her shoes.

"We were worried when the fetal monitor stopped reading your baby's heartbeat." There was an unmistakable note of censure in the nurse's tone.

"I haven't had a contraction in a couple of hours. The doctor said the baby's heart rate is great, so I thought I'd go see how my mother-in-law is doing."

And, then, she was going to ask one of her brothers-in-law to arrange for an escort home. She would call Tony on the way there and make sure he and Rusty were all right. She hoped they were. The last thing she wanted or needed was more blood on her hands.

She frowned, hiking her purse up on her shoulder and trying to shove the thought and the guilt away.

Maybe one day she would stop feeling as if she were responsible for the horrible things Martin had done.

Today was apparently not that day.

"We need to clear that with the doctor and with…" The nurse's voice trailed off, her gaze darting to the now-open door.

"The police?" Katie offered. "I know they're standing guard, but I'm not a criminal and I can go where I want."

"We still need to clear things with the doctor," the nurse

argued. "You had quite a scare this morning, and Dr. Ritter wants to be certain you and the baby are healthy."

"I'm as concerned as he is, but he has already assured me the baby looks great," Katie responded, anxious to get back to the quiet home she and Jordan had shared. Sometimes, if she allowed herself, she could still hear him walking up the steps and sliding his key into the lock.

Despite the long hours he'd spent on the job and the weekends she had often spent alone, she had always run into his arms when he returned home.

She missed that.

She missed him.

"Is everything okay in here?" A uniformed officer peered into the room.

"Everything is fine, but I would like to visit my mother-in-law. If you wouldn't mind escorting me there, I would appreciate it."

"I'll have to check with the chief," he responded. She recognized most of the men and women in the NYC K-9 Command Unit. He wasn't one of them.

"Noah Jameson is my brother-in-law," she said. "I'm sure he wouldn't mind."

"Currently the chief is out in the field." Another officer stepped into the room, a yellow Lab on a lead beside her. Katie recognized her immediately. Brianne Hayes was new to the K-9 team. One of the few female officers in the unit, she had proved herself to be a top-notch handler when she had helped apprehend a bombing suspect a few months back.

"Can you contact him? I'm anxious to see Ivy."

"I can try, but…" Brianne hesitated, the look in her

eyes reminding Katie of the one she had seen in the faces of the officers who had informed her of Jordan's death.

"What's going on?" she asked. "Did something else happen to Ivy? Is she…worse than they originally thought?"

"She's fine," Brianne answered hurriedly.

"Did something happen to Tony?" Katie asked, her mind rushing in a direction she had been trying not to allow it to go.

She had been married to a police officer.

She knew the risks.

Every time Jordan had left the house, she had known there was a possibility he wouldn't be coming home. Over the past few months, that nagging worry had transferred to the other men in Katie's life—her brothers-in-law and Tony.

Brianne hesitated, her gaze jumping to the other officer. "He's fine."

Her answer was about as reassuring as the concerned look on her face.

"Then, why do you look like he's not?"

"You need to relax and not worry, okay?" Brianne responded.

"I would worry less if someone would tell me what's going on."

"There isn't much to tell. Martin Fisher hasn't been apprehended. The chief is out searching for him with other members of the team. Until I hear something different, I'd rather you just sit tight and wait here."

"The NYPD have been hunting for Martin since he escaped the mental hospital. There's no guarantee he'll be found tonight or tomorrow, and I can't remain in the hospital indefinitely. Besides, I'm not asking to leave. I'm just asking to visit Ivy." She wanted to leave, though, and if she could talk one of her brothers-in-law into bringing her home, that's exactly what she planned to do.

"I have to check with the chief, but if I can get in touch with him, I'll see if I can clear it. Just give me a few minutes, okay?"

"Sure," Katie conceded. She was too tired to argue. Even if she weren't, she would have allowed Brianne to do her job. She had too much respect for law enforcement to make trouble for any of the officers.

"Thanks." Brianne smiled, her eyes shadowed with fatigue, her auburn hair tucked behind her ears. Like everyone on the K-9 team, she had been burning the candle at both ends, trying to locate and apprehend Martin.

"I'll contact Dr. Ritter," the nurse added, walking out of the room as the officers left.

Katie waited until they closed the door, then dug through her purse until she found her phone. She scrolled through text messages from friends who had heard about the attempted kidnapping on the news and were worried about her. Former colleagues had called, and she had gotten a call from her pastor. She didn't listen to the voice mails. She'd do that later. For now, she had the information she wanted. Tony had not tried to contact her. That wasn't surprising, if he was still out searching for Martin.

But, she couldn't forget Brianne's hesitation.

Something was wrong.

She was sure of it.

She swung open the door, determined to get the truth.

Tony was there, hand raised as if he'd been getting ready to knock. His jacket and uniform shirt were off, and a thick bandage was showing beneath the short sleeve of his T-shirt. There were specks of blood on his forearm and a smear of it on his cheek.

But, he was on his feet and alive, Rusty standing beside him.

She was so relieved, she threw her arms around him, pulling him close before she realized what she was doing.

Tony had been hugged hundreds of times, and he'd given plenty of hugs. At Jordan's funeral, he had stood beside Katie, his arm around her shoulders, offering support, because he had known that's what his friend would have wanted.

Now, though, she was nearly nine months pregnant, her belly pressing against his abdomen, her arms wrapped around his waist. He felt the baby move, the tiny life demanding attention.

He had made a promise to Jordan, and he meant to keep it. He would make certain Katie and the baby were safe. Even if that meant going out to hunt for Martin with a bandaged arm.

Katie stepped back, eyes dark in her pale face. "Sorry."

"For what?"

"The hug." Her gaze jumped to Brianne.

"No need to apologize. We're family."

"You and Jordan always did call each other brother," she said, offering a half smile.

"We did," he agreed. She was obviously self-conscious about what had been a completely platonic hug.

"I was worried about you." She touched the edge of the bandage that covered his cleaned and sutured wound. "Are you okay?"

"Fine. I would have been here sooner, but Martin grabbed a teenager in the park, and he was wounded."

"Oh no! Will he be okay?"

"He has a cut on his cheek and is shaken up, but he'll be fine."

"And your shoulder?"

"Also fine, but Noah insisted I get checked out at the hospital and take a couple of days to recuperate."

"That doesn't sound like a bad idea."

"It wouldn't be, if Martin weren't still running free." He took her arm and led her back into the room. The less time she spent out in the open, the happier he'd be.

"I was hoping to avoid returning to the hospital room," she murmured, stopping just over the threshold.

"It's best if you stay here."

"So everyone keeps telling me, but I'd prefer to go check on Ivy."

"I spoke with Carter a few minutes ago. Ivy is doing well. She broke her wrist and has a mild concussion. They plan to keep her for observation, but she should be able to return home tomorrow."

"Poor Ivy. This is all—"

"Don't say it," he cut in.

"What?" she asked, raising one light brown brow

and eyeing him with a look she had probably used on her fifth-grade class when she was teaching.

"That it's your fault."

"If I hadn't—"

"Katie, we could all spend our lives thinking about what we could have done differently, but none of us can go back. You and I go to the same church. I've spoken to Martin a few dozen times, and I never would have imagined he was capable of murder."

"You're right. I know that."

"Then, stop feeling guilty for the actions of a sick individual. There is nothing you could have done to keep him from becoming fixated on you. Even if you hadn't gone out with him, he may still have stalked you. He's unhinged."

"Maybe so." She smiled, but her eyes were sad. They'd been that way since Jordan's death.

"Exactly so," he replied, and some of the sadness left her eyes.

"You're always a cheerleader, Tony, and I appreciate it. But, I'd appreciate it a lot more if you would bring me to see Ivy and then drive me home."

He should have refused.

Noah had already told him to get treatment and to return home to rest. There'd been nothing in his directives about visiting Katie or taking her home. But, Tony had never been one to blindly follow someone else's lead. He was off the clock, and he knew how to protect Katie.

He'd bring her up to see Ivy, and then he'd check in with Jordan's brother Carter, who was still recovering from being shot several months ago and had only just returned to the office part-time. The other two Jameson brothers, Noah and Zach, were hunting Martin while Carter stayed at the hospital with Ivy and their father.

"All right," he agreed.

Her eyes widened, and she offered the first real smile he had seen in months. "Really?"

"Did you think I'd refuse?"

"Everyone else has."

"I'm not everyone else."

He touched her shoulder, brushing aside a thick strand of hair. She looked exhausted, her cheeks hollow, her eyes red-rimmed. In the few years that he'd known her, she had always seemed energetic and enthusiastic, her outlook optimistic. She had a clear-eyed, pragmatic view of life that had attracted Jordan and intrigued Tony. He had grown up in a family filled with silence and unspoken resentment. His mother had gone to the grave bitterly resentful of his father's career. An NYPD homicide detective, Dillard Knight had devoted his life to law enforcement. He'd had little time for his wife or his only child. Even when Tony's mother had been dying of cancer, Dillard had spent more time working than he had at home.

Jordan and his family had been Tony's escape from that, and when Katie had entered the picture, the joy she took in the simple things in life had captured his attention. That may have dimmed after Jordan's death, but she had kept her focus on the future and tried hard to stay positive.

He didn't want that to change.

Not because of someone like Martin.

"It's going to be okay, Katie," he said.

"Ivy told me that right before Martin showed up," she responded, stepping away and walking into the hall.

He followed, staying close as they walked to the bank of elevators that would bring them up to Ivy's room.

Jordan had never been one to ask for much.

He was more likely to give than to expect to receive help.

Tony once again thought about how Jordan had pulled him aside on the morning of the wedding and asked him to look after Katie if anything happened to him.

*She's strong. She can go it alone, but I don't want her to have to. I know my family will be there for her, but I want to know that she'll have someone on her side who knows what it's like to grow up without a firm support system in place. She's like you, man—just looking for a place to belong. You two will understand each other better than any two people I know.*

Tony remembered the words as if they'd been spoken seconds rather than years ago, and he remembered his response. That he'd be there if Katie needed him. Always. For a lifetime. If that's what was necessary.

Right now, she needed him.

Whether she realized it or not.

For as long as that was true, he'd be there, ready to do what Jordan couldn't—keep her and the baby safe.

# FOUR

Ivy looked better than Katie had anticipated. Head bruised and arm in a cast, she was holding court in the hospital room, Alexander and Carter sitting on one side of the bed, the pastor and two friends on the other.

"Katie! What are you doing here?" Ivy cried as Katie and Tony walked into the room.

"I wanted to make sure you were okay," she responded, bending down awkwardly to kiss her mother-in-law's cheek. Her belly seemed to grow bigger every day, the baby's elbows and feet jabbing into her sides so often, she had begun to wonder if she was carrying a future dancer or gymnast. Jordan would have been happy with either of those choices.

*Whatever our children decide to be will be fine with me, as long as they're happy*, he'd whispered in her ear the night she had told him she was pregnant.

He had been ecstatic.

She had been, too, but she had also been worried about how soon after the wedding the pregnancy had happened. She had wanted another year or two of teaching before she had kids, but Jordan had been gung ho to begin a family. She had also wanted to work until right before the baby was born, but Jordan had thought it would be best for her to give her notice before the new school year began.

In retrospect, she had compromised a lot in the short time they had been married. She wasn't sure how she felt about that. She was certainly glad to be pregnant and happy she would be bringing Jordan's child into the world, but without teaching and Jordan, the days since his death had been long and empty. Time had stretched out, and it seemed to be taking eons rather than months for the baby to arrive.

"You wanted to see how *I* was doing? *You're* the one who is about ready to have a baby," Ivy exclaimed, laying a hand on Katie's abdomen.

She tried not to tense.

She loved Ivy. She understood the gift the baby was to the Jameson family, but she wasn't used to having a mother in her life, and the attention often made her feel awkward and uncomfortable.

Tony might have sensed that.

He stepped up beside her and leaned down to kiss Ivy's cheek, distracting her from Katie and the baby bump.

"How are you doing, Mom?" he asked.

Ivy smiled just as she always did when he called her mom. "Better than you, I'd say. What happened to your shoulder?"

"I had a run-in with the sharp end of a knife. Nothing a few swipes of antiseptic and a bandage couldn't fix."

"That's an awfully thick bandage for something that only needed a little attention." Carter stood stiffly, grimacing.

He had the same blue eyes as Jordan and a similar smile. Katie had not seen much of it since he'd been shot. He had recently gone back to work part-time, but the doctors weren't sure if he would ever be able to return in his full capacity.

That had to be weighing on him.

Like his brothers, he loved the work he did with the K-9 unit. Katie had no idea what he would do if he couldn't return to it full-time. He had his daughter, of course, and his fiancée, Rachelle. It wasn't like his life was empty, but she knew Jordan would have been devastated to lose his ability to work in law enforcement. She imagined any of his brothers would feel the same. She hadn't asked Carter. As wonderful as the Jamesons had been to her, she had not known any of them for very long. At least not long enough to ask deeply personal questions.

"I was thinking the same thing," Alexander Jameson said, still seated beside Ivy, his hand resting on her shoulder. The patriarch of the Jameson clan, he had a good head on his shoulders, an abundance of loyalty to his family and a calm demeanor that all four of his sons seemed to have inherited. "I take it you got that from Fisher."

"Unfortunately, yes."

"Does Noah know?" Carter asked.

"He's the one who insisted I get treated at the hospital. I wanted to keep searching for Fisher. Rusty and

I almost had him." He patted the Lab's broad head and scratched behind his ears.

Rusty seemed to smile in return, his head cocking to the side, his mouth open, tongue hanging out.

"There is an entire K-9 unit hunting for him. We'll get him. It's just a matter of time." Carter sounded confident. There was no reason why he shouldn't be. Martin couldn't stay hidden forever. Eventually, he would show himself again.

She shivered, crossing her arms over her stomach.

She had been trying not to dwell on what had happened that morning, refusing to allow her mind to go to the darkest places. The places where Martin was successful in his kidnapping attempt and hurt the baby.

"You're exhausted, Katie," Carter said, his voice filled with concern. "You should go back to your room."

"I'd rather go home. I still have a lot to do before the baby arrives."

"The baby won't know if pictures are hung or if all the baby stuff is put away," Alexander pointed out.

"I know, but I'll feel better if I get things done." And, she would feel better away from the hospital and the four sets of eyes that were watching her intently.

"Going home is probably not a good idea. Fisher knows where you live, and based on what happened today, he's been watching your movements," Carter said.

"He got to me in a medical center. I don't think I'll be any safer here than I will be at home."

"She has a point," Tony said, unexpectedly coming to

her aid. "If guards can stand outside her hospital room, they can stand outside her house."

"That's true," Ivy agreed. "And, if I were in Katie's shoes, I would want to be home. As a matter of fact, maybe I'll follow her lead and get myself checked out of here."

"No, you won't," Alexander said calmly. "You have a head injury, and you need to stay here for observation."

"I believe I make my own decisions about where I'm going and what I'm doing," Ivy retorted, her gaze sharp. Her words sharper. She ran a tight ship at the Jameson house, keeping the five Jameson men in line.

*Four.*

There were only four Jameson men remaining.

Grief washed over Katie like it had hundreds of times since Jordan's murder, and she swallowed back tears.

"You do. Unless you have a head injury. In which case, I make the decisions." Alexander pressed a kiss to Ivy's hand and smiled. "I don't know what I would do without you, Ivy. So, how about you let me have my way this time? If you don't, I'll be pacing our bedroom all night, checking on you every fifteen seconds to make sure you haven't fallen into a coma."

Ivy's expression softened, and she touched her husband's cheek. "Fine. For you, I'll stay."

The exchange was brief and sweet, the simplicity and beauty of their love evident in the gaze that passed between them. They'd been married thirty-five years and had weathered many storms together.

That is what Katie had imagined having with Jordan. Martin had taken that from her.

"I'm assuming you plan to escort Katie home?" Alexander asked, his gaze shifting from his wife to Tony.

"I'll escort her there, and I'll stick around until one of you arrives."

"That's not necessary," Katie began, but it was. She knew it. They knew it. "What I mean is you're injured. If you'd rather me stay here so you can go home, I'll understand."

"I would rather you be somewhere that feels comfortable and safe. If that's home, then I'm all for you being there. Ready?"

She nodded, kissed Ivy's and Alexander's cheeks, waved to Carter and the other people in the room, and followed Tony into the hall.

Neither of them spoke as they took the elevator to the lobby. When they reached the hospital's exit, Rusty nosed the ground near the door and sniffed intently.

"Do you think he smells Martin?" Katie asked, suddenly wondering if she were making the right choice. Maybe the hospital *would* be safer than her house.

She almost told Tony she had changed her mind, but he opened the door and gestured to a police officer who was standing near the curb. Long and lean, the man had a narrow mustache and coal-black eyes.

"What's up?" he asked, his hand resting on his utility belt, the leather creaking as he moved.

"I need another set of eyes while I'm walking to my car," Tony replied.

"I can be that." The officer smiled and moved in beside Katie. Neither man touched her, but she felt cocooned between them.

It took seconds to cross the parking lot and reach Tony's SUV, the police K-9 logo emblazoned on the side. She waited while he opened the passenger's side door and moved a bloodstained shirt and jacket from the seat.

"That's a lot of blood," she said as she tried to pull the seat belt across her lap. Her hands were as clumsy as the rest of her, trembling as she attempted to snap the ends of the belt beneath her belly.

"Not really." He brushed her hands away and snapped the belt into place, his knuckles skimming her abdomen. Her cheeks heated at the intimacy of it. Tony leaning in, his head bent close to hers, his hair tickling her chin.

She had never thought of him as anything other than Jordan's best buddy. Tony had been beside her since his death, offering help, support and comfort. She had appreciated that, and she had thanked him for it, but she wasn't sure she had realized until just that moment how much it had meant to her.

"Tony?" She touched his wrist before he could close the door. "Thank you."

"For the ride? Thanks aren't necessary." He smiled and would have closed the door, but she had learned a valuable lesson from the deaths of her parents and her husband: always say what needs to be said to the people you care about.

"Not for the ride. For everything you've done since Jordan's death. You've been a rock. I don't know what I would have done without you."

"You would have been just fine."

"Maybe."

He didn't reassure her. He didn't offer platitudes. He studied her face, his gaze skimming across the curve of her cheek and down the flushed column of her throat. "Based on what I have seen the past few years and what Jordan told me about you, I don't think you have nearly enough confidence in yourself."

"I have plenty of confidence."

"Then, don't sell yourself short. You would have been fine, Katie. You're tough and smart. Even if you had no one but yourself to rely on, you would be okay." His fingers skimmed her cheek as he tucked a few loose strands of hair behind her ear. Warmth she hadn't expected or wanted seeped into her blood.

She thought he must have felt that strange and unsettling spark of heat. His eyes narrowed and his hand dropped away. He stepped back quickly and closed the door without saying another word.

She rested her head against the seat's headrest, closing her eyes and telling herself she was overtired and overreacting. What she had felt was a product of stress and trauma. Of course, she would have strong feelings for the person who had saved her life. It was a normal and expected thing.

Plus, she was nearly nine months pregnant.

Hormones were raging. Emotions were heightened.

That was all there was to the heat in her cheeks and in her blood.

Cold air swept into the vehicle as Tony opened the back hatch and let Rusty in. The Lab huffed quietly as he settled down for the ride. When the driver's side door opened, Katie kept her eyes closed and her body relaxed. She was too tired to talk, and too confused to want to.

The engine started, and the vehicle pulled out, the soft purr of the motor soothing some of the tension from her shoulders and neck. The heat in her cheeks faded, the country music Tony had playing a pleasant backdrop to the quiet rumble of tires on pavement.

"You're a country music fan?" she asked. She had had no idea. Now that she thought about it, there were a lot of things she didn't know about him. He had spent a lot of time with Jordan and, by extension, Katie, but she had never asked him where he lived or what he enjoyed beyond dogs and criminal justice. She knew he liked fishing and hunting. He and Jordan had taken a few long-weekend trips to Maine to hike trails and track game.

She had never joined them.

Tony had invited her once, but Jordan had told him that she wasn't much of an outdoors person. It wasn't true, but she had not corrected him. Not in front of Tony and not later when she had had the chance.

Like so many other things in the past, that hadn't seemed problematic. She had been newly married and in love. She had assumed she and Jordan would have all the time in the world to learn about each other.

Funny how life was.

All of the things that were planned so carefully often coming to nothing, and all of the unexpected things taking their place.

The SUV bounced over a pothole, and she almost

opened her eyes, but she didn't feel like talking. The baby had finally quieted, and all she wanted to do was be quiet with her.

Katie wasn't asleep, but Tony let her pretend to be.

Her relaxed muscles were a nice change from what he had grown used to seeing these past several months. Since Jordan's death, she had been tense and nervous, her skin pale and her face gaunt. Aside from the baby bump, she had grown thin; her once-athletic body had become almost too lean. Like everyone else who knew her, Tony had been worried. Once he had realized exactly what had happened to Jordan and why, his concern had grown exponentially.

He should have apprehended Martin today.

He *would* have apprehended him if not for Martin's using that scared teenager as his personal escape plan. Rusty shifted in the back of the SUV, his head popping into view and then disappearing again. The Lab knew work had ended for the day. His K-9 vest had been removed and he had been allowed plenty of attention and pets from hospital staff. Like any good working dog, Rusty knew what was required. He didn't seek attention while he was on the job, but when he was off duty, he was a typical goofy, happy-go-lucky Lab.

Traffic was slow in the city, as always, and it took nearly forty minutes to drive to the Jameson house. A three-level home on a pretty lot in a quiet Queens neighborhood, the multifamily dwelling was exactly what Jordan and his family needed. Like so many other New York City dwellers, they coveted fenced backyards. From what Jordan had said, it worked out well. The dogs had a place to run, family was close, but not so close there wasn't privacy.

Tony found a spot just a few doors up from the house. He'd park in the driveway, but he wanted to leave that available for Alexander and Ivy. As soon as the car engine died, Katie straightened, her long blond ponytail sliding over her shoulder as she reached for the door handle.

"Thank you for the ride, Tony," she said, as if she thought he would let her out and then drive away.

"I was hoping for an invitation to coffee," he said, not wanting to remind her of the attempted kidnapping or the fact that Martin was still on the loose.

"From what I've seen, you're not much of a coffee drinker, so I think it's more likely that you want to check the apartment and make sure Martin isn't waiting for me there."

"You're right—on both counts," he admitted.

"You could have just said that. It's not like I'm not aware of the danger I'm in, and it's not like talking about it will break me." She reached for the door handle again.

"Wait until I'm out, okay?"

"Sure." Her hand dropped to her belly. She still had specks of blood on her knuckles. Her jeans were torn. Her hands were scraped raw. The fact that Martin had gotten so close to kidnapping her filled Tony with fury and with fear.

He jogged to the hatchback and released Rusty. The dog was as familiar with the Jameson house as he was with his own, and his tail wagged happily as Tony opened Katie's door and offered her a hand.

"Thanks." She allowed herself to be helped out of the vehicle, her gaze scanning the exterior of the house, the driveway, the sun-dappled shrubs near the corners of the yard.

"If it makes you feel better, I don't think he is brazen enough to show up here."

"Did you think he was brazen enough to show up at the medical clinic?"

"I hoped he wasn't, but I was worried that he might." He and Noah had agreed it was a possibility, which was why Tony had been driving past the medical center every few minutes. "The fact is Martin is mentally ill and unpredictable because of it. We're using every bit of man power and caution we can to—"

"Tony," she cut in tiredly. "I know all that. I've been told the same thing by every member of law enforcement I've spoken to."

"Sorry. Sometimes I forget to take off my law-enforcement hat when I clock out for the day." He smiled to try to lighten the mood, but Katie was digging keys from her purse and didn't seem to notice.

"I didn't realize the hat ever came off," she commented as she led the way through the front door and up the stairs to her apartment.

"If a police officer wants to have a pleasant home environment and a happy family, it should," he replied.

"Interesting." She tried to fit the key in the lock, but her hand was trembling, and she kept missing the mark.

"Why?" He took the keys from her hand and unlocked the door.

"I don't think Jordan had a hat. Either that or it was always on." She would have entered the apartment, but he pulled her back.

"I'll send Rusty in first. He'll know if anything is off." He released the dog, watching as the Lab trotted inside and paused in the small entryway. He sniffed the floor, then raised his head and scent-checked the air. When he plopped down on the carpet in the living room, Tony knew the place was empty.

"Looks like he's making himself at home," Katie murmured as she stood in the doorway, her arm pressed against his, her body leaning just a little in his direction.

Before Jordan's death, she had seemed perpetually optimistic, her cheerful good nature making her a favorite with the K-9 unit. She had been the spouse who had brought Christmas cookies and holiday candy to the station, who had bought treats for the dogs and remembered everyone's birthday. She seemed to have faded since Jordan's death, her glossy hair brittle, her eyes shadowed and red-rimmed. Tony wasn't sure if it was Jordan's death or the pregnancy that had sapped so much of her energy.

"This is like a second home to him." He nudged Katie into the apartment, walked in behind her, locked the door, and then peered into all of the rooms and out each window, focusing particularly on the backyard below. The late afternoon sun had finally broken through the cloud cover, painting the grass with gold highlights. There were no footprints pressed into the earth near the fence line, no sign that anyone had been lurking near the property while the Jamesons were away.

Still, Tony felt uneasy, and he stood by the window for a moment longer, waiting for someone to step around the side of the house, for a shadow to move where one shouldn't, for Martin to show himself.

"Is everything okay?" Katie asked, and he finally turned away and walked back toward her.

"Fine, but you look exhausted. Why don't you go lie down? I'll put the crib together."

"With a bandaged shoulder? I don't think so." Her hands settled on her hips, and she looked like a Victorian schoolmarm, hair just a little messy, eyes blazing as she tried to take control of an unruly student.

"Your inner teacher is coming out."

She blinked and then, to his surprise, chuckled, her hands falling away from her hips. "Jordan used to say that to me every time I put my hands on my hips when we were…discussing things."

"Discussing? Is that the same as arguing?" he asked as he walked into the galley-style kitchen and opened the fridge. There wasn't much in it. Orange juice. Eggs. Milk. Cheese.

"Not when you're a newlywed," she replied. "If you're looking for a meal, you may have to go elsewhere to find it. Ivy and I planned to go grocery shopping after my appointment today."

"I'll go for you, after the Jamesons get home. For now, how about I make you an omelet?"

"I'm not hungry."

"The baby might be."

"The baby is sleeping." She pulled out a chair and sat at the kitchenette table, her stomach bumping the wood.

It wasn't his responsibility to get her to eat, so he poured a glass of juice and set it in front of her.

"Thanks for not pushing the food issue. Everyone I know seems to think a good meal will solve my problems."

"Maybe they just don't know what else to offer you," he suggested, taking the seat across from her.

"Probably not. There really are only so many things a person can say to a twenty-six-year-old pregnant widow. I suppose *eat this* is one of them." She smiled and took a sip of the juice.

"*I'll put together the crib* is another."

She chuckled again. "You're good at that, Tony."

"What?"

"Making me laugh." She pushed away from the table and stood. "Seeing as how I am exhausted and don't have the energy to do it myself, I'm going to do what Mrs. Henderson was always telling me and *not* look a gift horse in the mouth. If you want to put the crib together, I'll be happy to let you do it."

"Mrs. Henderson?"

"My last foster mother. I lived with her until I turned eighteen. She was a retired schoolteacher. Tough but kind."

"I didn't realize you were in foster care." He felt like it was something he should have known. Jordan had said a lot of things about Katie. He'd spoken about her intelligence, her caring nature and her optimistic outlook, but Tony couldn't remember him ever mentioning Katie's past.

"It's not something I talk about much."

"Is there a reason for that?" he asked, curious despite himself.

"There's not much to say. My parents died in a car accident when I was ten. Neither of them had any surviving family, so I was shuffled into the foster system." She shrugged as if it didn't matter, but he knew it did. He had lived through his own rough childhood. He knew how hard it was to break the old habits of silence and self-protection.

"That is a difficult thing for a kid to go through."

"It could have been worse. None of my foster homes were horrible or abusive. I wasn't mistreated. But, it was...lonely." She shrugged again. "When I found out I was pregnant, I prayed that God would allow Jordan and I to be around for our child through all the ups and downs of her life. Through the tough things that happen during childhood and adolescence. Through the chaotic teenage years. On into adulthood, because I miss that. Not having parents to turn to for the big things and the small ones. I don't want my child to ever feel alone. Maybe God was sleeping that day." She smiled, but the sadness was still in her eyes. Only, now, he understood it a little bit better.

"God never sleeps, but sometimes He has reason to say no. Maybe this is one of those times." He knew she didn't need the reminder. From what he had seen, Katie's faith had remained rock-solid after Jordan's murder.

"I've been reminded of that a few dozen times recently. But..."

"Like the omelet, the reminders aren't something you need right now?"

"Something like that. I'm exhausted. I'm going to lie down. Thanks again…for everything."

She walked down the hall that led to three bedrooms and a bathroom. Tony waited until he heard her door shut before following. The door to the guest room was open. He walked past without looking in. He had stayed at the house a few times before Jordan and Katie married. He knew the layout. The nursery was just across the hall from the master bedroom.

He moved silently, while Rusty's paws clicked against the hardwood floor behind him. Photographs lined the walls on both sides of the wide hallway, muted sunlight streaming through a window at the far end. As far as Queens apartments went, this was a good-sized one. The bedrooms were small but not tiny, and the living room was large and functional. The kitchen was narrow but still had an eat-in area. Jordan had once told Tony he would be content to stay there for the rest of his life. He had loved the city, and he had loved working for the NYPD.

If his life had not been cut short, he would have continued on his career path, striving to make a difference in the community he loved.

"This shouldn't have happened, brother," Tony murmured as he walked into the nursery. Jordan had not been around to choose the paint color or the bedding. He had had no part in picking the crib, which was still in a box in the middle of the floor. It didn't seem fair or right that a good, honest man was dead and his murderer was alive and free.

God's plans were always best, but that didn't mean accepting them was always easy.

Tony sighed, pulling his utility knife out and using it to open the box. It shouldn't take long to put the crib together. When he was finished, he'd go online and find a grocery-delivery service to have food delivered to the house.

He couldn't change the past, and he couldn't bring Jordan back, but he could do that.

# FIVE

Despite the discomfort of her pregnancy, Katie fell asleep. She woke to darkness and the soft sound of someone snoring. She reached across the bed to wake Jordan. She had done the same dozens of times before. Only now, instead of encountering Jordan's warm, muscular shoulder, her hand met empty air.

Because, of course, Jordan wasn't there.

Of course, his side of the bed was empty.

She was alone, yet she could hear someone snoring. She flicked on the bedside lamp, her heart pounding frantically. Someone was in the room, and the only person she knew of who might wander into her house and fall asleep like he belonged there was Martin.

He was *that* delusional and, if he had found his way into the house, she needed to find a way out.

Now!

She jumped from the bed and stumbled over something that was lying beside it. She went down on her knees and tried to jump up again, but her body was heavy, her movements uncoordinated.

She would have screamed, but her mouth was dry with terror.

She struggled to her feet, tried to take a step forward, but the thing that had tripped her blocked her path. Chocolate fur, dark eyes and a fuzzy face, Rusty watched her expectantly, his doggy grin chasing away her fear.

"Rusty! What are you doing in here? Did your handler leave and make you stay here to protect me?" She scratched his broad head, and his tail wagged happily.

Tony appeared in the doorway. "Actually, he was whining at your door. I knocked, but you didn't respond, so I opened the door to check on you. He slipped in and made himself comfortable by the bed." Tony stood on the threshold, his hair mussed, a five-o'clock shadow giving him a rugged, outdoorsy look. She had seen him like that before. He and Jordan had often watched football together or tossed balls to their dogs out in the yard on the weekend. She had loved sitting in the kitchen, sipping tea and watching through the window. Jordan's K-9 partner, Snapper, had enjoyed Rusty's company as much as Jordan had enjoyed Tony's.

The apartment had been too empty since Jordan's death. Snapper had gone missing the same day, and Katie had felt the absence of the loyal dog almost as keenly as she had felt the absence of her husband.

Her life had been full.

Now it seemed barren, every day stretching into the next with nothing but a few visits from friends and family to fill them. She tried to stay positive, to look toward the future and the birth of the baby with excitement and joy, but even that was tainted by the loss of the only man she had ever loved.

"Are you okay?" Tony asked.

"Fine," she murmured, kneeling ungracefully so she could run her hands over Rusty's warm coat. His tail continued to thump, and her eyes burned with tears.

She wanted her life back. The one she had so carefully planned and prayed about. The one that she had been so eager to step into. She wanted to go to bed at night knowing she wouldn't wake up alone in the morning. She wanted to make enough coffee for two and set the table for more than one. She wanted the things she had dreamed of during the long years of moving from foster home to foster home.

"Katie," Tony said quietly, crossing the room and crouching beside her. "You don't have to pretend to be okay."

"I'm not pretending," she lied, her focus still on Rusty.

He touched her chin, urging her to look at him. "Then, why are there tears in your eyes?"

"Because this wasn't the dream," she admitted. "This wasn't the answer I wanted to my prayers as a kid."

"I'm sorry," he said, staring into her eyes as if he could read her sorrow and heartache, and as if he understood it.

"I know," she said, that feeling she had had in the SUV welling up again as she continued to look into his eyes.

The air seemed to fill with it—a palpable tension that he must have noticed.

He stood, offered her a hand and then pulled her to her feet.

No more staring into her eyes.

He was all business, walking to the window to close the shades. "It's probably best to keep the shades drawn for a while."

"I guess that means they haven't apprehended Martin?"

"Unfortunately, it does." He ran a hand over his hair, smoothing the thick strands. "Noah called about an hour ago to say they were calling in the teams and regrouping. We'll meet tomorrow to discuss a plan of action. In the meantime, you'll have twenty-four-hour protection."

"Provided by the K-9 unit?"

"Yes. Currently, keeping you safe and apprehending Martin is our top priority."

"I'll have to thank whoever Noah sends to play bodyguard. Hanging around the house, waiting for something to happen, isn't going to be fun for someone who is used to being on the move."

"You can thank me by keeping the shades closed and staying away from the windows. I don't think Martin would harm you, but the less he knows about which room you're in and what you're doing, the happier I'll be."

"You?" She wasn't quite able to hide the surprise and uneasiness in her voice.

"It makes the most sense. I'm off on medical leave for a couple of days because Noah insisted, but my shoulder is fine. So, I'll take the first few shifts while other members of the unit pound the pavement and see if they can locate Martin."

"But…you're not supposed to be working," she protested.

"It sounds like the idea of me being here bothers you," Tony said, studying her face, probably seeing all kinds of things she would rather he didn't.

"Of course, it doesn't," she lied.

"You don't have to worry about what people will think, if that's what's bothering you."

"Think about what?" she hedged, because she *was* worried. But, not about that.

When Jordan had been alive, Tony had been the trusty sidekick. The guy her husband relied on when he needed help with home-improvement projects or yard work. The die-hard bachelor she had enjoyed setting a place at the table for when he came for a visit.

She had never looked at him as anything else.

Now, though…

Something was changing; their relationship was shifting from one that orbited around Jordan to…what? Friendship? Mutual respect? Affection?

She wasn't sure, but in the nearly nine months since Jordan's death, she had stopped seeing Tony as his bachelor buddy and begun to see him for who he was—a strong, driven, compassionate man who would do anything for the people he cared about.

She wasn't sure how she felt about that.

Disloyal? Alarmed? Worried.

"I thought you might be worried about what your neighbors will think if your deceased husband's best friend suddenly begins spending too much time at your place," he responded.

"I've never cared about what the neighbors think," she murmured, turning away and walking into the hall.

He followed. "Then, what are you worried about?"

She couldn't tell him the truth—that she was worried about the way she had felt when he had touched her cheek and when he had looked into her eyes.

"Everything. Ivy. Martin. All the K-9 handlers who are trying to find him. You." She added the last because it was true, and because she knew he would misunderstand the reasons for her concern.

"I can take care of myself, Katie, so don't waste any energy worrying about that."

"I'm worried about Snapper, too," she responded, glad to have the conversation on safer ground. "Has anyone been able to get in touch with the man who adopted him from the shelter?"

"Not yet, but we spoke to a neighbor who is taking in the mail and watching the house while he is out of town."

"If he's out of town, that would explain why he hasn't been in touch." She walked into the kitchen and put the kettle on to boil. She had given up coffee during her first trimester, when just the thought of it had turned her stomach. Now, she relied on tea to fuel her energy.

"It doesn't explain why he was able to adopt a microchipped police dog," Tony replied, a hard edge to his voice. Like everyone else on the K-9 unit, he had been putting in extra hours to search for the German shepherd. The dog had been spotted in Queens after Jordan's death, and Tony had scoured neighborhoods close to where he had been seen.

He had come up empty, and Katie knew that had bothered him.

"Did the shelter check for a microchip?" she asked. She had been so focused on Martin's escape, she hadn't asked many questions when Snapper had been spotted on an adoptable-pets search engine that the canine team had been perusing in the months following his disappearance.

"They are supposed to check every animal that comes in, but there is no record of that happening in Snapper's case. Which makes me wonder if someone knew who he was and skipped that part of the process on purpose."

"Why would anyone do that?" She opened the fridge to get milk for her tea and was shocked to see the full shelves and drawers.

"It costs a lot of money to train a dog like Snapper, and there are plenty of underground operations that would love to take advantage of his very expensive education."

"You're talking about someone who works at the shelter alerting one of those operations that a police dog had come in?" She was still staring at the contents of the fridge, her mind half on the conversation, half on trying to figure out how the empty shelves had suddenly filled.

"It's possible. Could be a volunteer there for just that purpose—to scout out high-value dogs. It's also possible that Martin somehow got rid of the chip or corrupted it."

"I hope you're wrong about someone at the shelter being shady." Jordan would have been devastated if the dog he had worked with for countless hours were being used for criminal activities.

"Me, too, and I probably am. More than likely, there was just a mix-up when Snapper was brought in. The microchip was overlooked, and he was adopted out before anyone realized it. He's a great dog, and if I had seen him in a shelter, I would have taken him home in a heartbeat." He stepped up behind her, his hand resting on the still-open refrigerator door. "Looking for something?"

"Trying to figure out how my empty fridge became full."

"I had a delivery service come bring a few things."

"You didn't have to do that, Tony," she said, grabbing the milk and moving away.

"Yes, I did. The night of your wedding, Jordan asked me to promise to look after you if anything ever happened to him. I never break a promise."

She withheld a gasp. She hadn't known that Jordan had asked such a thing of his best friend. She hadn't thought he would have had the foresight to be concerned about what might happen if he were killed in the line of duty. He had been a man who had liked to live in the moment, and he had lived each moment fully.

Now, that she knew, she understood Tony's constant attention since Jordan's death. The fact that he had been by her side so often, checking in and making sure that she was doing okay? It was part of the obligation he felt to his best friend.

No wonder Tony was here.

And, no wonder he'd ordered groceries and put them

away. He was stepping in and doing what he knew Jordan would want him to.

Knowing that shouldn't make her feel disappointed. She should be pleased that Jordan had been thinking about her future on their wedding day, that he had been preparing for whatever might come.

She was pleased.

But, that…awareness she'd noticed—*felt*—between them…? It was really just Tony Knight feeling the weight of the promise he had made. Understanding that didn't change anything. At least, it shouldn't. He was still Jordan's best friend. They still had their love for Jordan in common. He had still been there for her through the hardships of the past few months.

"Always is a long time," she murmured, refusing to meet his eyes. She didn't want him to see her confusion or her…disappointment? Maybe she did feel that. Just a little.

"I realized that when I made the promise," he said.

"Maybe, but I doubt you realized he would die. None of us were expecting that."

"I didn't expect it, but that doesn't mean the promise isn't valid."

"Tony, you don't have to feel obligated to me." The kettle was boiling, and she lifted it, poured steaming water over a tea bag and then added some milk.

Her hands were shaking again, the thought of Jordan pulling his best man aside to ask for such a huge favor making her heart ache. They had never discussed what would happen if he were killed in the line of duty.

It wasn't something she had wanted to think about. Let alone discuss.

"Helping you isn't an obligation," he countered.

"Then what is it?"

"It's friendship."

"I know how close you and Jordan were, but he wouldn't expect you to stand by a promise like that. You have a life to live that doesn't include his widow and child."

"I'm not talking about my friendship with Jordan. We're friends, too, Katie."

She met his eyes and could read the sincerity in his face. "We are, but I don't want to be your obligation. I don't want to be the reason you work too hard and spread yourself too thin."

"You're not an obligation," he said, stepping closer, his hands settling on her shoulders. "You're a reminder that life goes on after we're gone, and that the legacy we leave behind really does matter."

He was staring into her eyes again, and she could feel warmth spreading across her cheeks.

She wanted to look away, but she was caught in his gaze, remembering all of the times Tony and Jordan had sat on the couch, watching television while she worked on lesson plans at the kitchen table. Tony had always been the one to ask if the volume was too loud. He'd been the one to offer to bring her a soda or cook her a meal. If she were honest with herself, she would admit he had been more concerned for her needs and comfort than Jordan had been.

Rusty barked, and the sound was so unexpected,

Katie jumped, hot tea sloshing over her knuckles. She nearly dropped the mug, her scalded fingers burning as she set it on the counter. Rusty was barking ferociously. Hackles raised, tail stiff, he stood near the living room window, his head between the curtains and the glass.

"You okay?" Tony nearly shouted to be heard above the dog's frantic warning.

"Fine. It's nothing some water won't cure," she responded, putting her hand under the faucet and running water over it. "What is Rusty barking about?"

"I'm not sure, but how about you go in the bathroom to do that?" he suggested, tugging her away from the sink and the window above it.

"You don't think Martin is out there, do you?" she asked, her attention jumping to the darkness beyond the window. The sun had set hours ago, and all she could see was the shadowy outline of the six-foot privacy fence that surrounded the yard. It would be difficult for someone to climb but not impossible.

A light flashed, and the small storage shed that abutted the fence burst into flames, the blaze shooting outward and lapping at the branches of an old elm that stood in the center of the yard.

Shocked, Katie jumped back, and Tony's arms wrapped around her as she stumbled and nearly fell.

"Get your cell phone, go in the bathroom, lock the door and call 911. Don't open the door until I get back." He gave her a gentle nudge toward the hall, hooked Rusty to the leash and walked to the door.

She was still standing at the end of the hall, feet planted on the floor, heart galloping.

"I'll lock this door. You get your phone and call 911," he said again. "I'll be back as soon as I can." Tony stood with his hand on the doorknob, his dark eyes staring into hers.

He wouldn't walk out the door until she moved, and the longer she stayed where she was, the more likely the fire would burn out of control and that the person who had set it would escape.

Someone *had* set it.

There was nothing in the shed that would have spontaneously combusted. And, there was no one who would have set it except for Martin.

She swallowed down her terror and forced herself to nod.

"Be careful," she said, and then she turned and ran for her phone.

Tony didn't wait.

There wasn't time.

He knew exactly what had happened, and he knew why. Martin had set the fire, hoping to draw Katie out of the apartment. He wasn't going to get what he wanted. But, if Tony was quick, Martin might get what he deserved—a trip back to the psychiatric hospital and a trial before a jury of his peers.

He looked out the peephole, scanning as much of the exterior landing as he could. There was no sign of Martin. That didn't surprise him. Martin was unbalanced, but he wasn't stupid. He knew how to keep a low profile. He also knew New York City. He was good at using public transportation to move quickly through the city.

He had escaped the mental institution. He had escaped the attention of the police for weeks.

Tony didn't want him to escape again.

"Find!" he commanded, unhooking Rusty from the lead.

Rusty took off, bounding down the stairs, barking wildly.

Firelight flickered on wooden fence posts as the dog jumped at the gate, trying to open it and get into the backyard. Tony had the key to the lock that held the gate closed, but he knew Martin had not entered the yard that way, and he doubted he would exit there.

"This way," he commanded.

Rusty loped after him as he raced to the corner of the fence and plunged through the thick hedges that surrounded the neighbor's property.

He could hear someone crashing through the foliage ahead of him, and he picked up speed as he called out for the perpetrator to stop. Rusty flew past, his dark coat gleaming in the exterior lights of the neighboring houses.

A dozen yards ahead, a dark figure clambered over a wrought-iron fence and darted toward the street. Rego Park wasn't the suburbs; the yards were small, the houses packed close. Tony couldn't risk taking a shot at the fleeing figure. Not until he was sure there weren't any innocent bystanders nearby.

"I said *stop*!" he called, the faint sound of sirens joining the quiet rumble of neighborhood traffic as he and Rusty followed the perp.

The man reached the road and darted toward a light-colored four-door Ford. He stopped when he reached it, the streetlights illuminating his familiar face. Tall and muscular with a rock-solid build he had earned on construction sites, Martin Fisher didn't look anything like the staid, suit-wearing guy Tony had seen at church.

He scowled as he met Tony's eyes, reaching under his jacket and pulling out a gun. "You need to stay away from Katie," he growled.

"Or what? You'll murder me the same way you murdered Jordan?"

Martin didn't speak. Didn't blink. Just aimed the gun and fired.

But Tony was already diving to the side, calling Rusty back as the bullet slammed into a car parked a few feet away.

"Martin! Put your weapon down and give yourself up," Tony commanded, Rusty pressing close to his side, both of them prone near the edge of the street. Tony had his gun in hand as Martin jumped into the car and slammed the door.

He gunned the engine as Tony took aim at a back tire.

It exploded, bits of rubber flying as the car fishtailed, straightened and accelerated. Not forward as Tony had expected. Backward. Straight at him.

He rolled to the side, scrambling out of the way, Rusty stuck to his side like glue. The Lab might be a search-and-rescue dog, but he was trained to function in volatile, dangerous situations involving firearms. Currently his most important job was staying out of the line of fire.

They moved in sync as Tony ducked behind a parked vehicle and aimed for the back window of Martin's car. He fired a round, as Martin reversed direction again and sped away. Glass shattered. The car fishtailed again, but Martin kept going. He was escaping, and that was something Tony couldn't allow to happen.

Martin needed to be stopped.

Before he made good on his plans to abduct Katie.

He called for Rusty to heel as he sprinted into the middle of the road and followed the damaged vehicle down the street. He lost sight of it as it turned the corner, but he didn't think Martin would be able to keep going on the blown tire. He'd have to stop eventually. When he did, Tony planned to be there.

# SIX

Sirens and smoke.

If Katie forgot everything else about the evening, she thought she would still remember the faint whirring of the sirens and the acrid scent of smoke that seemed to be filling the bathroom.

She pressed her palm against the door, checking for heat because of the fire. It was cool to the touch, and so was the old-fashioned metal doorknob. Tony had been gone for twenty minutes. She doubted that was long enough for the fire to spread from the shed to the house, but the yard wasn't large, and the leaves of the elm would make perfect tinder for the flames. A few errant sparks, and who knew? The house could catch fire, and she could be trapped.

She had already called 911.

Based on the sound of sirens, help had arrived.

Martin wouldn't stick around with so many first responders outside.

Would he?

Tony had been right when he'd said that Martin was unpredictable. There was no way to know what he might do, but sitting in a burning building was a more certain death sentence than getting out of one and running into Martin.

She unlocked the door and eased it open, listening for any movement in the apartment. When she heard nothing, she stepped into the hall, her heart sloshing in her ears as she eased along the wall and made her way to the living room. The scent of smoke was thicker there, as the wood frames on the windows that looked out over the backyard were warped enough to let cold air seep in during the colder months.

She flipped off the kitchen light and walked to the window. A half dozen firefighters were there, holding a hose that was spraying the smoldering remains of the shed. The elm seemed untouched, its wide trunk and broad branches dark against the evening sky.

A dog barked, and when someone knocked on the front door, she hurried to answer it, looking through the peephole first.

Her brother-in-law Noah.

She yanked open the door. "Noah. What are you doing here? I thought everyone was still at the hospital."

"We were on our way back when the call came in. I sent Mom, Dad, Carter and Ellie to a hotel and came straight here to pick you up. Zach is outside with Eddie. We have a team looking for and collecting evidence. I wanted to take you over to the hotel before I join the team."

"I'm fine here," she said. "Tony was with me, but he left when the shed lit up to try to catch Martin."

His gaze dropped to her abdomen, and she knew exactly what he wanted to ask.

"The baby is fine, too. No more contractions. Go do what you have to do and stop worrying. Tony will be back up soon."

"It's tough not to worry when the guy who killed my brother is wandering around Queens, causing trouble." He ran a hand down his jaw and shook his head. "We're going to find him, Katie. I promise you that. And when we do, we're going to make sure he is punished to the full extent of the law."

"I know." She tried to smile, wanting to reassure him because she knew how much he and his family had suffered these past few months. They were grieving just like she was. Yet somehow they continued doing their jobs and seeking justice.

"Okay. Sit tight for a little longer. Try to relax. I'll check in when we're finished." He opened the door and called for Scotty as he stepped onto the landing. He looked tired; his eyes were shadowed, and a few fine lines were starting to show near them.

"Noah," she said, stepping into the doorway and touching his arm. The cold fall air carried the stench of smoke and a hint of moisture that could turn into rain or snow.

"You need to stay inside. We have no idea where Martin went after he drove away. Until we find him, you're going to be under twenty-four-hour guard."

"Tony told me that, and I appreciate everything the K-9 unit has done to keep me safe. I also want you to know I appreciate you and your brothers on a personal level. You have done more than I ever could have asked or expected, and it means a lot to me. It's hard knowing Jordan won't be here for his child, but knowing that you and your brothers will be…" She swallowed a lump of grief and forced herself to keep going. "That makes it a little easier."

"Jordan chose well, Katie. We all think that, and we're glad you're part of the family." He pulled her into a quick bear hug and then stepped away. "Close the door and lock it. Stay inside."

She did as he had asked, then walked back into the living room, her body humming with useless adrenaline. She was a good friend, a good teacher and a good cook, but she wasn't a police officer. She had no training when it came to dealing with men like Martin, and she knew the best thing she could do—the smartest thing—was to stay where she was and wait for the experts to do their job.

She had never been good at waiting, though, and she walked back into the kitchen and looked out the window. The hose had been turned off, and there was nothing but a blackened carcass where the shed had once been. The grass all around it was burned, the ground a black scar where it had once been.

She had done this.

Not intentionally.

Not with her own hands.

But, with her actions and her choices.

No matter how many times she told herself it wasn't true, no matter how many people told her, she couldn't make herself believe it.

"Stop it," she muttered, walking away from the window and out the kitchen. She needed to stop dwelling on things she couldn't change. She needed to trust that God's plan was working out. She needed to move into the future. No matter how faltering and slow her steps.

And, that meant getting ready for the baby's arrival.

She had been avoiding it for weeks, but the hint of smoke in the air, the knowledge that tomorrow could bring more troubles, was enough to spur her to action.

She stepped into the nursery, her pulse jumping in surprise as she saw the crib put together and standing against the far wall. Tony had unpacked boxes of baby clothes and put them in the dresser. The diapers were in the drawer of the changing table. A small basket hooked to the side contained baby wipes and lotions. He had taken the cardboard boxes out to recycle and carried the rocking chair from the guest room, where she had stored it.

*Stored* it?

Hidden it. The antique rocking chair had been in Ivy's family for three generations. She had rocked her sons to sleep in it. She had rocked Carter's daughter, Ellie, in it. Two months after Jordan's death, she had asked Alexander to carry it up to Katie's apartment with a note that said they were redecorating the guest room, and she was hoping Katie would accept the chair as a gift for the baby.

Katie hadn't wanted to.

She had argued that one of the Jameson men should have it, but Ivy had been insistent. Noah, Carter and Zach were crowded enough in their apartment with all of Ellie's things; they didn't need to add more. Plus, Ivy wanted Jordan's child to have it. A reminder that Jordan had once been young and lively and loved.

Just thinking about that had made Katie's eyes burn with tears.

She had put the rocking chair in the guest room, closed the door and left it there, because she hadn't wanted to think about what it would be like to talk to her child about the father who would never be there to read a book, watch a game or give advice.

Now, the rocking chair was in the corner of the room, the standing lamp Zach and his wife, Violet, had purchased for the nursery beside it. She had bought a three-shelf bookcase months ago, and Tony had assembled that, too. He'd even slid all of the books she had been given by friends and church members into place there.

The room looked like what it was—a space for a baby. One who would be well loved and well cared for by an entire tribe of family and friends.

*That* was what she needed to think about.

Not what wouldn't be, but what would.

"It's going to be enough," she whispered, lifting a children's Bible that was sitting on top of the bookcase. She had clung to her faith through a lot of hard times, and she wasn't going to give up on it now.

But, lately, it was hard to see God in the details of her life.

Her cell phone rang, and she pulled it from her pocket, glancing at the caller ID before she answered. She didn't recognize the number, but Ivy and Alexander had gone to a hotel. It was possible they were calling from there.

"Hello?" she said breathlessly, dropping into the rocking chair, the baby wriggling around as if the phone had woken her.

"You're going to have to forgive me, darling," Martin said, his voice as smooth and cold as a snake's skin.

"What did you do?" she asked, jumping up from the chair and rushing to the back door. She opened it and looked down into the backyard, hoping to see a police officer or one of her brothers-in-law.

The yard was full of officers.

"Go back inside, darling. It's too chilly to be out without a coat," he said, and her blood ran cold, her body numb.

"Where are you?"

"Not far. I tried to get to you, but there are too many people around. I would ask you to come to me, but I don't want you to tire yourself when you're so close to giving birth to our child."

"Where. Are. You," she repeated, her heart racing so fast, she felt light-headed and woozy.

She lowered herself to the floor of the deck, afraid she might pass out and fall down the stairs.

"Close enough to know you're safe, but too far to help you escape. I'm sorry, my love. I should have planned the fire better. I thought it would burn slowly and that your...friend would come and investigate."

"Martin, you need help," she murmured, her head still spinning, her ears ringing.

She had never passed out before, but she had the horrible feeling that she might.

"I need you. I need our child. I need the life we planned together."

"We didn't plan anything. This isn't your child. It's Jordan's. You know that. Just like you know that there is nothing between us. There never has been. There never will be."

"You have obviously been listening to Jordan's family. They've brainwashed you," he snapped, his tone hard. "Once you're with me, you'll remember how much we love each other."

"Please. Turn yourself in. Get help. Stop stalking me."

"*Stalking?* Is that what you call my devotion? You're an ungrateful wretch. You know that? If you're not careful, I'll take our child and leave you behind." He ended the call, and she sat where she was, holding the phone to her ear.

"Katie?" Tony called.

She glanced down and saw him jogging toward the stairs to the deck, Rusty on heel beside him.

"What are you doing out here? Noah said you were in the house, waiting for him to return."

He hurried up the stairs, but she didn't stand to greet him. She was still clutching the phone, her throat so tight with terror, she didn't dare try to speak.

She was afraid that if she did, she would start screaming and never stop.

"Katie?" he said again, dropping down beside her and taking the phone from her hand. "What's happened? What's wrong?"

She shook her head, because she couldn't get the words out. Couldn't tell him the threat Martin had made. The thought of a madman kidnapping her child made her feel physically ill.

"Come on. Let's get you inside." He helped her to her feet and ushered her into the apartment.

"Sit. Before you pass out." He held her arm as she lowered herself to the couch. Then, he patted the cushion beside her.

"Place," he said, and Rusty jumped up and settled his warm head on her knee.

Tony set the phone on the end table and disappeared for a few minutes, returning with the guest-room comforter in his arms. He wrapped it around her shoulders, then bent so he could look into her eyes. "Tell me what happened. I'll take care of it."

If anyone else had said it, she would have brushed it off, but she was looking into the darkest eyes she had ever seen, reading sincerity and concern in them, and she knew that, if he could, he really would take care of things.

"I'm probably overreacting," she finally managed to say, because she thought she probably was.

There were dozens of firefighters and police officers on the property. Martin wouldn't be able to get to her. But, it wasn't what could happen now that had her terrified. It was the future—the unborn baby who would make an entrance into a world where Martin was wandering free.

"You aren't the kind of person who overreacts to things."

"I didn't used to be. The pregnancy has changed me."

"Don't do that, Katie," he said, wrapping the comforter tighter around her shoulders, his fingers skimming the sides of her neck. She could imagine—if she let herself—leaning into his warmth, allowing herself to find comfort in his arms. Just the thought made her heart ache with guilt and sadness.

She had loved Jordan.

She didn't expect to ever love anyone else.

She certainly had no intention of filling the empty spot he had left with his best friend.

"Don't do what?" she murmured, focusing her attention on Rusty. That was easier than looking into Tony's eyes.

"Downplay your experience. You're levelheaded and smart. Pregnancy hasn't changed that. If you're worried, then I have every reason to think I should be, too."

"I'm not..." She stopped herself. She was worried, and Tony was right. She had never been the kind of person to blow things out of proportion or make mountains out of molehills. Being in foster care had forced her to be resilient, to take each day as it came and to hold her emotions in check. "Okay, I *am* worried. Martin called."

"Your home phone?"

"My cell."

"You gave him your number?"

"No, but it's in the church directory."

"We'll try to trace the call. If he called from a landline, that should be easy. If it's a disposable cell phone, it will be a lot more difficult."

"I'm sure it was a cell phone. Unless he broke into a house somewhere nearby."

"Nearby?"

"He said he could see me. He even told me to go back inside because it was too chilly to be out without a coat."

His eyes flashed, his jaw tightening. Unlike Jordan who had had a perpetual smile, Tony tended to look gruff and a little unapproachable. "Stay here. I'm going to talk to Noah."

"There's something else, Tony," she said as he opened the front door.

"Go ahead."

"He said that if I didn't cooperate, he would take my baby and leave me behind." Her voice broke on the words, the fear she had finally gotten under control threatening to escape again.

"He's not going to get the baby. He's not going to get you. We're going to keep constant watch and make sure of that." He stepped out of the apartment, into the hallway, signaling for Rusty to stay.

The Lab settled down next to Katie again.

She patted his head, her heart still beating too rapidly, her stomach hollow with anxiety.

She wanted to believe that things would work out.

She really did.

But, her track record for losing people she loved was high, and she didn't think she could count on anything other than things happening exactly how they were going to.

Outside, people were still calling out to each other. Men. Women. All of them working as a team.

Inside, though, it was just Katie and a dog that belonged to someone else.

Loneliness wasn't a state of being; it was a disease,
and it could destroy a person if allowed to.

She wouldn't allow it.

She had a life to live and dozens of years of memories to make with the child she and Jordan had created
together.

She wouldn't let Martin take that from her.

She wouldn't let him destroy the one thing she still
had.

She touched her belly as the baby kicked and squirmed.

"Don't worry, sweetie," she said. "It's going to be
okay. I promise."

The K-9 unit fanned out across the neighborhood,
searching yards, outbuildings and vehicles for Martin.
If what Katie had said was correct—and Tony had no
reason to doubt it—the escaped murderer was close
enough to see the Jameson house, to see what Katie
had been wearing and to know exactly where law enforcement was. That put him at a decided advantage.

But, the K-9 unit had dogs and manpower on its side,
and Tony had no intention of sitting idle while the rest
of the K-9 team hunted for the very dangerous and de-
luded man.

Despite his shoulder injury and orders to take a few
days off, he had teamed up with Officer Reed Branson and his bloodhound, Jessie. Reed had used a pil-
low taken from Martin's room at the mental hospital
after he had escaped as a scent article, allowing Jessie

to sniff it until she knew exactly what trail she should be following.

"Where's Rusty?" Reed asked.

"Staying with Katie for now," Tony explained. "Rusty will alert Katie to any danger faster than she would be able to notice anything on her own. I feel better with that safeguard."

Reed nodded, and they got to work.

Nose to the ground, Jessie followed the fence line and made her way into a neighbor's yard. She stayed there for several minutes, nosing a large rosebush that sat close to the neighbor's house. The earth beneath it was obviously disturbed, recent rain making it soft enough for footprints to be left in the soil.

Tony flashed his light on the area, his heart jumping when he saw a clear footprint between the house and the bush. "He must have been here for a while," he said. "The print is deep."

"Agreed. And, look at this." Reed pointed to what looked like blood on one of the branches.

"Not a smart idea to hide in a rosebush."

"Not smart, but it gave him a great view of the street and the side of the Jameson house. He may have been hoping Katie would return home alone. Or, with someone who wouldn't be able to help if he made another attempt at kidnapping her." He put in a call for the evidence team, then set a flag near the rosebush. "Martin is smart, but his delusions are causing him to make mistakes. His mistakes are our opportunities."

"Agreed," Tony said, standing back as Jessie began following the scent trail again. Nose to the ground, ears brushing grass and fallen leaves, she covered ground quickly with her long, muscular body. Like most bloodhounds, Jessie didn't give up on a scent once she had it. She moved quickly as she followed it across the neighbor's yard and out into the street where Tony had confronted Martin. She stopped there, circling a few times before she found the scent again.

She trotted along the road in the direction Tony knew Martin's vehicle had gone. "Do you think she's catching scent from his car?" he asked.

Reed shrugged. "It's possible. She's got a great nose, and the scent is fresh. She'll lose it if he's gone too far, though."

"He didn't. I blew out one of his tires."

"Yeah. I thought I heard that over the radio. You think he abandoned the car and circled back?"

"I can't think of any other way he would have been able to see Katie."

"He really *is* making mistakes. This neighborhood is crawling with police. There is no way he's going to escape the dragnet we've set for him."

"He's escaped the other ones. The subway station isn't that far from here. All he has to do is make it there, and he's gone," Tony pointed out.

"All we have to do is stop him," Reed responded, picking up speed as Jessie barreled around the corner of a street three blocks from the Jameson place. She trotted across a lawn and up a driveway that led to the back of a three-level house that had been turned into apartments. Like many in the neighborhood, it had a small paved area in the back for tenant vehicles.

Tony spotted the car immediately, parked bumper-to-bumper with a sporty Toyota. Its back tire was missing, its rim was bent and its back window was shattered.

Jessie made a beeline for it, baying loudly as she jumped up against the side of the car to look inside.

"Off," Reed commanded, and the bloodhound fell back, taking her place beside Reed as he pulled his firearm and moved in.

Tony moved in tandem with him, easing toward the car, watching for any sign that Martin was still there.

The area was still and quiet but for the muted sound of traffic that drifted between the old houses. The air was tinged with smoke. It was still early, and lights were on in neighboring properties—a television was visible through the open curtains of the next-door neighbor's house. People were in their homes, going about their evening rituals, unaware that a deranged killer had been feet away and might still be close by.

Tony reached the car and glanced inside, knowing before he checked that Martin wasn't there. A jacket was lying on the front seat, with a flip phone sitting on top of it.

"I would venture a guess that that's the phone he used," Reed muttered, his tone reflecting the frustration the K-9 unit had been feeling for nearly a month. Martin had murdered their chief, been captured and somehow escaped. The fact that he was still free was both frustrating and infuriating.

"He must have parked the car and walked to an area where he could observe the Jamesons' house, then returned after he made the call. He left the jacket purposely," Tony added. "To draw the dogs here."

"And left the phone to let us know he was one step ahead," Reed added. "But, leaving the jacket was another mistake. We can use it to get Jessie started again. She can track him from here."

"I have a feeling she'll scent-track straight to the subway station."

"I do, too, but Martin seems to be getting more delusional and less rational. It's possible he's staying close." Reed snapped a photo of the car's interior, called for the evidence team and set another flag. Then, he lifted the jacket with gloved hands and held it for Jessie to sniff.

When she had the scent, he placed it back in the car and gave the signal for her to search.

She took off, racing through the backyards of several houses before darting across a driveway and out into the road. She had the scent, and it was a strong one. Whether or not they would reach Martin before he escaped Rego Park remained to be seen, but Tony had never been a quitter. From the time he was young, he had gone after what he wanted with single-minded determination.

Right now, what he wanted—*all* he wanted—was to apprehend Martin Fisher before he had a chance to go after Katie again.

# SEVEN

The walls were closing in, and there wasn't a whole lot Katie could do about it. In the week since Martin had set fire to the shed and called her cell phone, she had been housebound, as requested by the K-9 Command Unit, her brothers-in-law, Ivy, Alexander and Tony. The Jamesons had refused to stay at the hotel once they knew the house was sound and that Katie had insisted on staying. Everyone who knew anything about the case had begged her to stay inside, where she could be guarded and protected.

She hadn't needed convincing.

She would do anything to protect her unborn child. Even stay inside for long days and long nights.

Now, though, she was restless, pacing the living room, the shades drawn, the door locked and bolted, her overnight bag sitting next to it.

Just in case.

She had kept her appointment with Dr. Ritter the previous day. Accompanied by Noah, Zach and their dogs, she had arrived at the medical center and departed from it without incident.

She *had* felt watched, though; the skin on the back of her neck had tingled as she maneuvered her ungainly body into Noah's SUV. Martin had called a few minutes after they'd pulled out of the parking lot.

*You are glowing, my love. Carrying our child suits you*, he had said. *What did Dr. Ritter think? Will the baby be coming soon?*

She had been terrified.

Just like she was every time her phone rang.

She had tried to keep him on the phone, stretching the conversation out in the hopes that it could be traced. When he abruptly disconnected, she had felt drained.

The K-9 unit had converged on the clinic, combing the area for signs that Martin had been there. They had found nothing except a scent trail that had led from the clinic to a queue of taxis waiting in front of a hotel.

As far as Katie knew, they still had not found the taxi driver who had given Martin a ride.

She sighed as she walked to the kitchen and opened the fridge. It was nearly midnight. She wasn't hungry, but she felt restless and lonely and a little afraid.

Even knowing there were two armed police officers watching the house and that her brothers-in-law were in the apartment above her couldn't ease her worry and fear. Martin had threatened to take the baby. No matter how many times she told herself he would never have the opportunity, no matter how many people reassured her, she couldn't shake the feeling that he would make good on his threat.

She was trying to give everything over to God. She really was, but it was difficult to trust that He wouldn't let anything happen to the baby when He had allowed something terrible to happen to her parents and to Jordan.

*It's all part of God's plan. You just have to have faith.*

How many well-meaning people had said that to her?

And, how many times had she stopped herself from telling them that her faith had not saved her parents and it had not saved her husband, and she had no reason to believe it would save her child?

God's plans and His ways were a mystery she couldn't solve. She knew He was good. She knew He had her best interest at heart. She knew she could count on Him to guide her steps. But, she did not know if He would spare her baby, if He would keep Martin away or if He would give her the peaceful life she so desperately craved.

The home.

The family.

The future she had prayed for.

Her phone rang, her pulse jumped and the baby shifted as the sudden spurt of adrenaline hit. The stress couldn't be good for either of them, and she tried to calm her breathing and slow her heart rate as she glanced at the caller ID.

It was an unknown number, but she knew who was calling.

It was nearly midnight. Everyone else she knew was either asleep or working. Even if they weren't, they would assume she was tucked in bed, resting for the upcoming birth.

"Hello?" she said, bracing herself for the smooth, slimy voice of the man she had grown to despise.

"Tell him to leave!" Martin screamed, his rage palpable.

"What are you talking about? There's no one here," she responded, taking out a cell phone Noah had provided and then hitting the quick-dial function to contact the precinct and let the dispatcher know Martin was on the phone.

"You know who I'm talking about, Katie. Don't play dumb."

"No. I don't." The baby twisted and squirmed, obviously as distressed by the conversation as Katie.

"Knight. He is trying to steal you from me the same way Jordan did. I don't want to murder someone else. I'm a peaceful guy. One who just wants to marry the love of his life, raise a family and enjoy the beautiful things God has provided for him."

"Tony isn't trying to steal me—" Katie attempted to say, but Martin started ranting, his words filled with bitter fury.

"And, if anyone tries, the same thing will happen to him that happened to Jordan. You tell Knight that, you hear me? Tell him!" He disconnected.

She was so shocked, she stood where she was, phone still pressed to her ear, heart hammering against her ribs.

She had known he was mentally ill. She *had*.

But, she had not known just how deep his delusions went.

She finally disconnected and shoved the phone into the pocket of the suit jacket she had put on a few hours ago. The pinstriped blue suit was one of the few items of Jordan's clothing she had kept. He had worn it the night he had proposed, and she had not been able to let it go.

She lifted the second cell phone to her ear and spoke to the dispatcher for the first time since she had made the call.

"Were you able to trace it?" she asked, her voice shaking.

"We have a ping from the cell phone that originated the call," the dispatcher replied. "I've already contacted the chief. He's gathering a team. Stay where you are until he contacts you."

"Okay. Thanks," she said, glancing at the ceiling as the floor joists above her head creaked.

Carter was awake. Noah and Zach were at work.

Ivy and Alexander were away for the weekend, spending a few days with friends before the baby arrived, so Carter would stay with his daughter, Ellie, while his brothers went to hunt for Martin.

*Please keep them safe*, she prayed silently.

She didn't know what she would do if another Jameson brother was killed by Martin.

Someone knocked on the door, and she hurried to answer it.

Or, *tried* to hurry.

She was moving more slowly than ever, the pregnancy heavy and cumbersome, her belly huge. Rather than running, she waddled, reaching the door breathless and tired, a stitch in her side making her pause before she peered through the peephole.

She expected to see Noah or Zach, returning from

work and coming to check on her before they retired for the night.

Tony was there. Dark hair gleaming in the hallway light, jaw dark with five-o'clock shadow.

She unlocked the door and stepped back. Something in her chest went soft as he walked inside, Rusty padding along beside him.

"You look tired," she said without thinking.

"Three twelve-hour shifts in a row will do that to you," he responded, closing the door and sliding the bolt into place. "I was on my way home and decided to bring coffee for the guys pulling guard duty and to check on you. I heard the call go over the radio while I was talking to them. Martin called again."

It wasn't a question, but she nodded. "He knew you were here. He told me to tell you to leave."

"He's going to be disappointed to discover that I haven't."

"You should, Tony," she said, the cramp in her side worsening.

"Because you want me to go?"

"Because I don't want you hurt. Martin said—"

"Let me guess—you're his. He won't let anyone get in the way of the two of you being together. He already murdered Jordan, and he will murder again if anyone tries to take you away from him."

"Something like that," she replied, bending over as another, sharper cramp shot through her abdomen.

"You okay?" he asked, taking her arm and leading her to the couch.

"I tried to run to answer the door. The baby didn't

like it," she responded, easing onto the cushions, the jacket billowing out as she sat.

She suddenly felt self-conscious for wearing it, as if it were tangible proof that she wasn't healing and moving on.

"Jordan wore this the night he proposed," she said, smoothing her hand down one of the too-long sleeves.

"I know. I was there—remember?"

"How could I forget? You wore a tux and a frilly pink apron while you served dinner from the gigantic picnic basket you somehow carried into Central Park." She smiled at the memory, because it was a good one. The way the fading sunlight had washed the grass and trees in a golden haze and the late-summer air had wrapped around her as she had walked hand in hand with Jordan. Her surprise when he had taken her to a small clearing where a blanket had been spread on the soft summer grass. Her laughter when Tony had appeared wearing a well-fitted tux and a pink apron.

"I rented the tux, and I didn't want to get anything on it. When I mentioned that to Ivy, she offered the apron. I wasn't going to wear it, but Jordan was a nervous wreck and I thought it might lighten the mood." He smiled, his gaze soft with the memory.

"Jordan nervous? That's hard to believe," she replied, her breath catching as another cramp made her stomach spasm.

"You two hadn't been dating that long when he proposed. He was worried you might say no."

"That definitely doesn't sound like the Jordan I knew."

"No? What was he like? The Jordan you knew, I mean." Tony's attention was focused on her rather than on his phone or the television or one of the dozen other things Jordan had spent his time looking at when she had tried to talk to him. He had always been tired from long days on the job, and she had always made excuses for him, because they had been newly married and she had not wanted to think that the pattern of behavior was one that would follow them throughout their marriage.

She hadn't been happy, though. Not with that part of their relationship.

The thought made her feel disloyal, and she shoved it away.

"Too confident to be worried about being turned down by one of the dozens of women he had dated in his life." She kept her tone light, not wanting Tony to think she was criticizing the man they had both loved.

"He loved you, Katie. He wanted to spend the rest of his life with you. The proposal and your answer meant everything to him," he said quietly. "I hope you know that."

"Of course, I do," she lied, pushing up from the couch and walking into the kitchen. "Are you hungry? Do you want me to make you something before you leave?"

"You're changing the subject," he pointed out.

"Because there is nothing more to say."

"I have a feeling there is. Was there trouble between you and Jordan before he died?" he asked bluntly.

She shouldn't have been surprised.

As caring and compassionate as Tony was, he had always been a straight shooter. From what she had seen, he didn't play games, didn't beat around the bush and didn't mince words.

"No. Of course not."

"But, something *was* bothering you."

"What if something was? Jordan wasn't perfect, and neither was I. We both did things the other didn't like."

"Such as?" he asked, refusing to let the subject drop.

*A dog with a bone* was how Jordan had described Tony. *And the perfect cop because of it.*

"I worried too much about what his family thought of me, and he… He was more focused on work than on building our relationship. At least, that's how it felt to me." She shrugged, and the nagging ache in her side swelled with pain again.

She rubbed the area but refused to look away from Tony's searching gaze.

"I can see how you might have thought that," he finally said. "Jordan was devoted to his job, and he had a difficult time breaking away from it. My father was a police officer, and he was the same way."

"Your mother didn't mind?"

"She hated it. By the time she died of cancer, I'm pretty sure she hated him, too. But, my father was also mean. He didn't care that Mother was lonely. He didn't care that he never saw me. All he cared about was looking good to his buddies on the police force."

"I'm sorry," she said, touching his arm, feeling firm muscle beneath his jacket and knowing she should let her hand drop away.

Instead, it rested there as he tugged her a step closer, her belly bumping his abdomen as he continued to look into her eyes. Something sparked between them, a hint of attraction that could have meant nothing or everything.

"I can't tell you that Jordan wouldn't have stayed committed to his job, but I can tell you this—he was also committed to you. You would have made it, Katie. The two of you would have raised a bunch of kids and grown old together, and I would have been the sidekick, looking on and wondering why I hadn't ever had the guts to give love a go." His gaze dropped to her lips, and his jaw tightened.

He stepped back, putting space between them that she should have wanted but didn't.

"Is there a reason why you haven't?" she asked, hoping he didn't notice the huskiness of her voice or the reluctance with which she moved away.

"I don't ever want to be to another person what my father was to me and my mother," he replied, the honesty of his answer making her want to reach out to him again.

And, that scared her.

Her stomach cramped again, and she grabbed the counter.

"Are you sure you're okay?" he asked, taking a step toward her.

"Fine. It's just been a long week, and I need some rest. Drive carefully on your way home," she responded.

"I told Noah I would stick around until he and Zach

returned. Go ahead and lie down. I'll be here if you need anything."

She nodded, grateful he'd be here—at a distance, while she rested in her bedroom. There was a lot about Tony Knight she hadn't known. Sides to him. His past. Including the promise he'd made to Jordan to watch over her. He was doing just that. Making good on the promise to his late best friend. Following orders from his chief. Maybe the awareness she kept feeling between them was all in her mind.

But, she didn't think so.

"All right. Thanks." She would have hurried away, but she had learned her lesson. She moved slowly instead, making her way down the hall and closing herself in her room.

She sat on the bed, waiting for the cramp to ease.

She had been in false labor the previous week. She knew what contractions felt like. These weren't them, so she lay down, still fully clothed and wearing Jordan's suit jacket, closed her eyes and tried to sleep.

Tony knew he needed to be careful.

Katie was a beautiful and intelligent woman, and he wasn't going to pretend he hadn't noticed. But, she was also his best friend's pregnant widow. That made her off-limits.

The truth was she would have been off-limits anyway. He never dated "forever" kind of women. He dated women who were as interested as he was in keeping things light. No expectations. No commitment. Just nice evenings out and pleasant conversations. That had always been enough for him.

Although, lately...

Lately, he had been wondering if his hard-core opposition to marriage had been built on faulty reasoning. As he had watched one member of the K-9 unit after another find love, he couldn't help thinking that he had as good a chance as anyone of making a lifetime commitment work.

He wasn't his father.

He had always known that.

As committed as he was to his job, he made time and space for the people he cared about.

The fact was he was getting older. His friends were married or getting there, having children or planning to. And, he was still living a bachelor's life, sitting down for meals alone or with families that weren't his.

He frowned, lifting a framed photo from one of the end tables. Jordan smiled out at him, arm around Katie, blue eyes alive with happiness. Jordan had never believed that Tony would remain single forever.

*You'll meet your happily-ever-after*, he had said a few weeks before his murder. *And, when you do, I'll be the first one to say I told you so.*

"I wish you could," he murmured, setting the photo back in place, grief a hard knot in the middle of his chest.

He walked over to the living room window and looked out, hating that Martin was skulking in the bushes somewhere, watching. Probably right now. The guy was likely getting more furious that Tony hadn't heeded the warning to stay away from Katie. Furious and delusional were not a good combination. Tony always watched his back, but he'd be vigilant now. Both for Katie's sake *and* his own.

Martin's last call had come in three hours ago. Tony had received no updates on the team's search, which meant there had been no changes. No sightings and no capture. He wanted to be out there, searching with Rusty, but Katie's well-being was everyone's top priority. Leaving her alone—even when she had two officers stationed outside—was not an option.

Her bedroom door opened, the soft creak of the old hinges warning him seconds before she appeared at the end of the hallway. She still wore Jordan's suit jacket, but her hair had come out of its ponytail and was spilling over her shoulders.

"Everything okay?" he asked, moving toward her.

"I'm not sure," she replied, her eyes dark blue against pale skin.

"Did Martin call again?" He hadn't heard a phone, but she might have had her cell phone's volume turned down.

"I think I'm in labor," she responded, the words so surprising it took a few seconds for them to register.

"Labor?" he asked. "As in the baby is coming?"

She grinned, some of the tension easing from her face. "You've known this baby was coming for a while. Why are you acting so surprised?"

"It's early."

"Only a couple of weeks."

"And, you have three brothers-in-law and two very

concerned parents-in-law who were supposed to be on scene when the big day arrived," he responded.

She laughed. "Don't sound so horrified, Tony. I can have one of the officers—"

"No." He grabbed her coat from the closet.

"You didn't let me finish."

"Because you don't need to have them do anything except follow us to the hospital. I'm driving you there, and I'll be there with you until you tell me to leave or until one of your family members shows up and boots me out." He dropped the coat around her shoulders and grabbed his jacket.

"Carter is upstairs. I can call him. Ivy and Alex are out of town, visiting friends, but Carter can probably find someone to sit with Ellie," she said, and he stopped frantically searching for his phone just long enough to meet her eyes. Despite her smile and laughter, she looked scared.

"If that's what you want, I'll be happy to sit with Ellie."

"What I want is for Jordan to be here," she replied.

"I wish I could make that happen for you." He tugged the edges of her coat closed and pulled silky hair from beneath its collar. "Do you want me to call Carter?"

She shook her head. "Ellie keeps him busy, and he needs his sleep. We can call him when I'm further along."

She reached for the small bag that sat near the door, and he took it from her hand.

"I'll leave Rusty here. He's good at the hospital, but

he already worked a full shift today and I'd rather let him rest. Do you need anything else?"

"Courage?" she responded.

"I can be that for you," he said, dropping his arm around her shoulders and ushering her out of the apartment.

# EIGHT

The baby arrived three hours after Katie checked into the hospital, the labor so quick, there was barely enough time to breathe let alone think about how nervous she was. True to his word, Tony had stayed with her, sitting beside the bed and holding her hand as things progressed. When it was time to push, he had asked if she wanted him to leave, but she had been gripping his hand too tightly to let him go.

She was glad for that.

Her daughter had not been born into the world with an audience that consisted only of medical staff. She had been born into a room that contained two of the people who had loved her father most.

Even now, an hour after Jordyn Rose Jameson had arrived, Katie's eyes filled with tears when she thought of that.

She blinked them away, not wanting Tony to ask questions.

He was still beside her, talking quietly to one of her brothers-in-law, his voice a soothing rumble that made her want to close her eyes and sleep.

She shifted Jordyn in her arms and ran her hand over the baby's soft brown hair. "You're beautiful, Jordyn Rose. Your daddy would be so happy if he were here."

"Yes, he would," Tony agreed, leaning closer so that he could look at Jordyn's face. "Noah is asking for a picture to show people at work. I said I would ask you."

"That's fine, but I'm a hot mess. Just take a picture of Jordyn." Even though she wouldn't be in the shot, she still smoothed her hair and straightened the collar of the cotton nightgown she had changed into after Jordyn was born.

"He would love that."

"Who?"

"Jordan. He would love that you gave your daughter his name. And, you aren't a hot mess. You two are the most beautiful mother and daughter I have ever seen." He lifted his cell phone and snapped three quick pictures.

"I'm pretty sure I told you not to take a picture of me." But, she didn't care that he had. Not really. Her daughter had been born alive and healthy. Ten fingers. Ten toes. Chubby cheeks and a rosebud mouth. Fine brown hair and a tiny button nose. Katie could not have asked for anything more than that.

"One day Jordyn Rose is going to be very happy that you have these photos, but if you would rather me not send the one with you in it to Noah, I won't." He smiled, and she felt that thing in her chest melt again, the solid mass of anxiety and grief that she had been carrying for so long seeping away.

"Go ahead and send them. I know everyone in the

K-9 unit has been praying for a healthy and safe delivery. I'm happy for them to see that their prayers were answered."

*Please, God, keep answering*, she prayed silently. *Keep protecting my daughter.*

"You look nervous," he commented as he sent the photo. "Worried about being a new mom?"

"Worried about Martin doing what he threatened and kidnapping Jordyn Rose," she admitted, kissing the baby's downy cheek.

"I'm not going to let that happen. The team isn't going to let it happen."

"I know." But, she was still afraid. "I just wish he had been apprehended."

"Me, too. Unfortunately, the dogs lost his scent at a bus stop. We're obtaining surveillance footage from the one we think he boarded, and we're hoping to discover where he got off. For right now, dogs and handlers have returned to the precinct."

"I know how much work everyone is putting into finding Martin. I wouldn't want anyone to think I'm not aware of it and grateful. It's just hard knowing that the man who murdered Jordan is still out there."

"I know." His fingers skimmed her shoulder, and his hand rested on her upper arm. She could feel the warmth of his palm through the thick cotton of her nightgown, and it felt so right and so comfortable that her eyes drifted closed.

"You're exhausted," he said quietly. "How about you let me hold the baby while you rest? I won't leave the room with her. I promise."

She forced her eyes open and looked at his familiar face. How had she never noticed the flecks of gray in his dark eyes, or how long his lashes were?

"Have you ever held a baby?" she asked, shifting her gaze before she could notice more.

"Not that I can remember, but there's a first time for everything, right?"

"You're not boosting my confidence in your ability," she murmured, kissing Jordyn Rose's head.

"I promise you, in as much as I am able, I will never let anything happen to her," Tony said solemnly.

And she knew he meant every word. That for as long as he could, he would be around to make sure that Jordyn Rose was safe.

"Okay," she said, because Tony had always been someone she could rely on. Even before Jordan's death, he had been there for her, rushing to the rescue anytime Jordan wasn't available.

Which, she had to admit, had been often.

She supported Jordyn Rose's head as she held the swaddled infant out for him.

His large hands slid across hers as he shifted the baby's weight and pulled her to his chest. He stayed there, the baby held closely, her head cupped by one of his hands, her body by the other.

"You look terrified," Katie said, oddly touched by the picture they made — tiny infant and large, gruff man.

"She's delicate, and I tend to be a bull in a china shop when it comes to delicate things."

"I watched a documentary that tested that idiom

once," she said, something warm and a little alarming filling her chest.

"Did you?" He was staring down at Jordyn Rose as if she were as delicate as a gossamer thread.

"Yes, and they discovered that a bull isn't all that destructive when let loose in a china shop."

"Good. Great. This little one and I should be just fine, then." He settled into his seat, Jordyn Rose close to his chest. "Man, she's beautiful," he whispered. "Jordan would be over the moon with love for her."

"I know." Her voice broke, and she closed her eyes, willing the tears away. This was a happy time. Not a sad one, and she didn't want to waste a second of it crying tears of sorrow.

"It's okay to cry, Katie. There isn't anyone who wouldn't understand why you're doing it."

"I know, but I don't want to cry tears of sorrow on the day of my daughter's birth. Maybe on her first Christmas or first birthday or the day she gets married. But, not today."

"That's a big jump from first birthday to wedding," he commented, and she knew he was trying to lighten the mood and take her mind off the one thing that was missing from this day.

The one person.

"I hear it goes by in a flash—all those years," she responded, her eyes still closed, exhaustion finally winning the war against her desire to stay awake.

"You blink and then she's grown," he agreed.

"Hopefully not that fast of a flash." The words were slurred, her body heavy with fatigue.

She thought she felt Tony's fingers skim across her cheek, but before she could decide if she had, she fell asleep.

Tony had never been part of something like this, and the miracle of the tiny life he was holding filled him with awe. He had heard from friends who had children that newborns were incredibly beautiful, but he had figured blind love had skewed their perspectives. He'd seen photos of their babies. The red faces, misshapen heads and squished noses had not been his definition of beauty, but he had oohed and aahed anyway.

Jordyn Rose, though… She was about as perfect as a human being could be. Tiny little fingers and toes. Cute little nose and chubby cheeks, she had stolen his heart the second the doctor had placed her on Katie's chest. He had been holding Katie's hand, her fingernails digging into his palm, his face so close to hers, he could see the blond tips on her brown eyelashes. He had not expected the baby to be plopped down, naked and pink and still speckled with blood, but that's exactly what had happened. One minute, Katie was red-faced with effort, and in what seemed like the next, a baby was lying on her chest.

"You're something else, sweetheart," he whispered, not sure if he was talking to the baby or to Katie. Both, in his admittedly exhausted opinion, were amazing.

Katie's cell phone rang, and he grabbed it from the table, answering before it could wake her. "Hello?" he said quietly, holding the phone with his shoulder so that he could keep two hands on Jordyn.

"Who is this? Why do you have Katie's phone?" a man said, his familiar voice sending a jolt of fury through Tony.

"Martin?"

"I asked who this is," Martin spat, hatred seething beneath the words.

"Tony Knight."

"I told her to tell you to go home. I know she doesn't want you around, so I suggest you do it."

"Here is what I suggest—go to the nearest police station and turn yourself in. That will make things a lot easier for you."

"For you, you mean?" He laughed, and the sound sent chills down Tony's spine.

"I'm not concerned about what is easy for me. I'm concerned about making sure you pay for what you did to Chief Jameson."

"Be careful, Knight. If you're not, your police buddies might wind up trying to make me pay for what I do to you." He disconnected, and Tony dropped the phone on the table again, frustrated by the helpless rage that filled him.

Martin should never have been able to escape the high-security mental institution where he had been held after his arrest, but he had knocked the guard over the head and made a run for it. If he had been a typical criminal, he would have kept going until he had put plenty of distance between himself and the law. Martin was anything but typical; he was unhinged and so obsessed with Katie, he had returned to Queens and begun stalking her.

So far, the NYC K-9 Command Unit had not been able to stop him. Public transportation made it too easy for Martin to move from location to location. Patrol officers had searched his apartment but found no hint that he had been there recently. Since then, foot and bike patrol had been making the apartment complex a regular stop during shifts. They had not seen the fugitive, but that didn't mean he hadn't slipped past them. He still had a key to the apartment, and the lease was paid up until the end of the year. That was unusual, but Martin had probably wanted to make sure he'd have access to his apartment even if he was caught. He'd clearly always planned to escape custody.

Jordyn Rose wriggled in his arms, her tiny fists batting the blankets that swaddled her. She looked like Katie, her features delicate, her skin pale, but she had Jordan's dark hair. The fact that she would never meet her father, that she would know him only through the stories that others told, made Jordan's death even more tragic.

Someone knocked softly, and the door swung open. Two officers were stationed outside the room, and Tony knew there was no danger of Martin getting past them. He stood anyway, the baby cuddled to his chest.

Ivy and Alexander Jameson walked in, and he motioned for them to stay quiet. Katie needed to rest, and he wanted her to sleep for as long as she could.

Ivy nodded and rushed across the room, tears streaming down her cheeks as she stared at the baby. "She's gorgeous," she whispered as Noah and his fiancée, Lani,

Carter and his fiancée, Rachelle, and Zach and his wife, Violet, entered the room.

"I was just thinking the same," he admitted.

"How is Katie?" she asked, her gaze shifting to the bed.

"Exhausted."

"It's been a rough nine months," Alexander said quietly, standing beside his wife, his arm around her waist, his gaze on Jordyn. "Noah said Katie named her Jordyn Rose."

"She did."

"It's a lovely name," Ivy murmured. "Do you think Katie would mind if I held her?"

"Of course not," he said, but he felt reluctant to let her take the baby from his arms. Odd considering he had never in his life imagined holding a newborn. He had never had a desire to do so. When friends had babies, he visited but kept his hands to himself.

"I can't believe she is finally here," Ivy said, brushing aside her tears and reaching for Jordyn Rose. "Ellie is going to be so happy to hear that her baby cousin has arrived! She'll want to buy *all* the frilly dresses and pink bows."

"She begged me to bring her this morning," Carter said, stepping close to his mother and taking a picture of her holding the baby.

Rachelle snapped a few photos of Carter standing next to Ivy and Jordyn Rose. Then Lani and Violet insisted on photos of their Jameson men beside Grandma and their newest niece.

Tony moved back, giving the Jameson family a

chance to coo over its newest member. Katie was still sleeping, her hair tangled beneath her head. He tugged the blanket up around her shoulders, concerned by her pale skin and the violet shadows beneath her eyes.

Since Katie was sleeping, Violet, Rachelle and Lani decided to head to the cafeteria for coffee and took orders. Tony could definitely use some coffee.

"Thanks for being here for her," Noah said, joining him beside the bed.

"That's what family does," he responded.

"I know, but I still wanted to tell you how much we appreciate it."

"You know what would be better than appreciation?"

"Martin locked up in a cell, facing a life sentence?"

"Exactly. He called Katie a few minutes before you arrived."

"And?"

"He wasn't happy when I answered. I have a bad feeling about things, Noah. The guy is totally unglued, and he has his sights set on a woman who has just given birth."

"You're not telling me anything I don't already know. We've put as much manpower on this as we can. The department is already stretched thin, and I can't devote the entire K-9 unit to Martin's arrest. If I could, I would."

"I know. You're talking to a member of the unit, remember?"

"Yeah." Noah ran a hand down his jaw and sighed. "I want him caught yesterday, Tony. He killed my brother. He's trying to kidnap his widow. He needs to be stopped, but he seems to always be a step ahead of us."

"He's getting cocky and making mistakes. He won't stay ahead of us forever."

"You're right. I just want this over. For Katie's sake and my parents'. For all of ours."

Katie stirred and her eyes opened as quickly as they had closed.

"The baby!" she cried, shoving aside blankets as if she intended to jump out of bed.

Tony touched her shoulder, gently holding her in place. "Hey, slow down. The baby is fine. Ivy has her."

She finally seemed to take in the room and the people who were standing in it. She sagged against the pillows, her skin so pale he could see every freckle on her nose and cheeks. "I was dreaming that Martin had taken her."

"We aren't going to let that happen," Noah said, taking a seat beside her as Ivy put the baby back in her arms.

"I know you're not. I know it was just a dream, but I don't know what I would do if it came true." Her voice broke, and the tears she had said she didn't want to shed slid down her cheeks.

"Don't cry, honey," Ivy exclaimed, rushing to wipe her face with a tissue. "Everything is going to work out. God will make certain of that."

Katie nodded, her gaze finding Tony's, her eyes filled with worry and heartache and hope. He wanted to tell her that Ivy was right and that everything really would be okay, but words weren't nearly as effective as action when it came to achieving a goal.

He motioned for Noah to follow him across the room. Carter and Zach joined them.

"I've been thinking about Martin and how easily he's been able to elude us," he said.

"Public transit, crowded streets, overabundance of scent pools with millions of scents mixed in," Zach said. "Even the best dog may struggle under those circumstances."

"I agree, but I don't think that's the reason Martin is able to stay hidden. He has to be going somewhere he doesn't think we'll look for him."

"Agreed," Carter and Noah said in unison.

"I think the most likely place for him to do that is his apartment."

"We've checked there," Noah reminded him.

"Immediately after he escaped. Since then, I don't think anyone from the precinct has been in."

"You may be right, but his landlord agreed to keep an eye on things and let us know if Martin showed up. We've also had patrol officers driving by the complex several times a day. Do you really think Martin would risk it?" Noah asked.

"The fact that we're asking that question makes me think he would. The way I see things, Martin tries to anticipate what we'll do and how we'll act. He has to know that we've been in the apartment, and he may assume that we won't go back unless someone tells us he's been there."

"His apartment *is* on the ground level," Zach said. "And there are plenty of windows in his unit. If he managed to break the lock on one, it would be easy enough for him to slip inside."

"I'll send someone there to check things out," Noah said.

"I'll go," Tony offered. "I need to get back to your place. Rusty is in Katie's apartment, and he's past ready for breakfast and a walk."

"You're not on shift today," Noah reminded him.

"I can be. If it means we find Martin more quickly."

"All right. Get Rusty, go home and eat, take a few hours to rest, and then go to the apartment. The superintendent should be able to let you in. If you find anything, let me know."

"I will." He glanced at the bed. Katie was nursing Jordyn Rose, her attention focused on the newborn. As if she sensed his gaze, she looked up and smiled, her expression open and inviting and soft.

"Are you leaving?" she asked, and he nodded, his throat tight with something that felt an awful lot like longing.

"Rusty is still at your place. I don't want to leave him there alone too much longer."

"You don't have to explain, Tony. You've been here for hours. That's way above and beyond the call of friendship."

"Not even close," he replied and then dropped a kiss on the top of her head. Her hair smelled like baby powder and flowers, and he wondered why he had never noticed that before.

"Do what the doctor and your family tell you, okay?" he murmured, his fingers grazing Jordyn Rose's downy head. He didn't want to leave. He wanted to stay right where he was, guarding Katie and the baby and watching as the mother and daughter bonded.

"I'm too tired to do anything else," she replied, smiling as he stepped away. "Be careful, Tony."

"I will be. I'll come back this evening. Just to make certain Jordyn Rose hasn't sprouted into a young adult and gotten engaged while I wasn't looking."

She chuckled, her laughter drifting into the hall as he walked out of the room.

# NINE

By early evening, Katie could barely keep her eyes open. She and Jordyn Rose had had a string of visitors. Friends from church, coworkers from her former school, officers from the K-9 unit. The Jamesons had stayed close; Jordan's brothers and parents had made sure she had anything and everything she might have needed.

Currently all she needed was sleep.

Her pallor, lethargy and high heart rate had alarmed the nurse, and Dr. Ritter had been called. He'd ordered blood tests, and when they showed severe anemia, she'd had a blood transfusion.

Guests had been shooed out, and Katie had insisted the Jamesons go have dinner while she was examined and treated.

Now she was alone, the baby lying comfortably in her arms. Jordyn Rose had not cried once since her birth. When she was awake, her eyes opened wide as if she were trying to take in every detail of the odd world she had suddenly found herself in.

Katie had known love before.

She had loved her parents. She had loved Jordan. She loved her in-laws. But, the love she felt for her daughter was something she had no words for. The strength of it had taken her by surprise. Even now, when she was so tired that she thought she might pass out, she didn't dare rest for fear of what might happen while she was sleeping.

Her phone rang, and she grabbed it, checking the caller ID before she answered. She had no desire to speak with Martin. The day had been eventful, and she wanted it to end as wonderfully as it had begun.

When she saw the caller was Ivy, she answered quickly. "Hello?"

"It's Ivy, dear. We got caught in rush-hour traffic and just now found a place to get some dinner. It's crowded. You know how Friday nights in the city are."

"Yes. I do," Katie said, stifling a yawn.

"I told Alexander that I should take a cab back to the hospital. I can stop in the cafeteria and grab something that we can share."

"Ivy, don't do that. Enjoy your family dinner."

"Honey, you're family, too."

"What I mean is that I don't want you to give up your plans to sit in the hospital and watch me and the baby sleep."

"Is our darling Jordyn sleeping?" Ivy asked, her voice soft with affection.

"She ate like a champ fifteen minutes ago, and now she's sleeping like one."

"Wonderful! And, what about you? Did the doctor find the reason for your anemia?"

"Nothing that he could put his finger on. Probably just the pregnancy."

"I'm glad to hear that, but I still think it would be a good idea for me to return to the hospital."

"Ivy, I would feel horrible if you did that. Your sons are always so busy. A family dinner is rare. Please just stay and enjoy yourself."

"Are you sure?"

"Absolutely."

"All right. We'll see you when we're finished here. Give Jordyn Rose a kiss for me."

"I will," she promised, ending the call and setting the phone on the bedside table. She could have agreed to Ivy's return. Her mother-in-law would have been thrilled to hold the baby while she slept, but Katie might need help when she returned home and she didn't want to be a burden to the only family she had.

She stared at her daughter's face, and she couldn't help thinking about her parents and how excited they would have been to welcome their first grandchild. They would have been just as thrilled as the Jamesons. Maybe more so because Katie was their only child.

A tear dropped onto Jordyn Rose's face.

Katie brushed it away, sniffing back more that were threatening to fall.

Someone knocked, and the door opened, the shift nurse bustling in with a tray of what looked like soup and juice. "Dr. Ritter ordered you a liquid meal. I told him you hadn't been hungry today, and he wants you to eat."

"I'm still not hungry," Katie said, holding Jordyn Rose closer as the nurse set the tray on the table.

"If you want to be released tomorrow, you need to get your blood count up and some food down."

"Will soup keep my blood count up?" she asked, eyeing the bowl of soup. It looked like chicken noodle. Any other time, she would have been happy to eat it.

Currently, she was so tired, she couldn't imagine lifting a spoonful to her lips.

"No, but rest might. You're exhausted. Your body has been through a lot. *You've* been through a lot. Not just today. We're talking months of stress."

Of course, she knew Katie's story.

It seemed everyone Katie met did.

"I think I need sleep more than I need food."

"Take this from a woman who has had six children— you need both. When you get home, you're going to be doing the late-night and early-morning feedings on your own. You'll be burning the candle at both ends, trying to keep up with the baby's appetite while you also try to keep your house in order. Tell you what—we don't have regular nurseries like they did when I had my children, but when a mom is really tired, we can take the baby to the nurses station—"

"No. I don't think that's a good idea," Katie said, her heart pounding frantically at the thought.

"Hear me out, hun," she responded. "No one is allowed on this floor without checking in downstairs. We've got guards posted at the elevator, checking visitor identification. Little Jordyn Rose won't be more than six inches from a nurse at any given time. As a matter of fact, she'll probably be held the entire time she's with us. We love newborns." She smiled reassuringly, and Katie's resistance began to fade.

She knew that everything the nurse said was true. She had been assured by the doctor and the nursing staff, as well as by the Jamesons and Tony, that every precaution was being taken.

And, if Martin did find a way onto the floor, he would assume the baby was with Katie and try to gain access to her room. If she was asleep and he walked in, he could take the baby and she would be none the wiser.

The thought terrified her.

"You're sure she won't be left unattended?"

"I have been working here for thirty years. In all that time, we have never left an infant unattended. Nor have we lost one."

"All right," Katie agreed reluctantly, afraid if she didn't, she would fall asleep and wake to find the baby gone. "She ate twenty minutes ago. She'll probably want to eat again in a couple hours."

"We'll bring her back as soon as she starts fussing. Don't worry about that."

"Okay." Katie kissed Jordyn Rose's head and her cheek. "Love you, sweetheart. Mommy will be right here if you need me."

She handed the baby to the nurse, her body humming with nervous energy as she watched the woman place Jordyn Rose in the bassinet and roll it away.

"She'll be fine," Katie whispered to the empty room.

She told herself she believed it as she ate a few

mouthfuls of soup, drank a couple sips of juice and finally let her eyes drift shut.

After visiting Martin's last known address, Tony had received a call from dispatch with information regarding an apartment owned by Martin's great-aunt. She had died several years ago, and probate court records showed that she had left the apartment to Martin. It was an unexpected lead and one Tony was anxious to follow up on.

It was dark by the time he arrived at the apartment complex—a tall brick building surrounded by large homes that had been there since the 1920s. Tony walked the perimeter of the building, letting Rusty sniff the ground. The Lab tugged impatiently at the leash, pulling Tony to a ground-level window on the west side of the building.

Rusty stopped there, nosing the ground and huffing gently, his ears and tail nearly quivering with excitement.

"What is it, Rusty?" Tony asked, studying the window and the ground beneath it.

Rusty whined, his scruff raised, his dark eyes focused on the window. He wanted inside, and Tony was going to get him there.

He walked back to the apartment entrance and rang the buzzer. Several minutes later, the super appeared.

"What can I do for you, Officer?" he asked as he opened the door.

"I'm investigating the murder of—"

"That police officer? Heard about it on the news.

Don't know what that has to do with this apartment complex, but I'm happy to help, if I can."

"We're looking for a guy by the name of Martin Fisher. We have reason to believe he owns a unit here." Tony pulled out a photo of Martin and handed it to the super.

"This the guy who shot the cop?" the super asked.

"Yes."

"Can't say I've seen him around. Most of the residents here are older folks who bought long before I started working here."

"His great-aunt owned the unit." Tony offered the name and, the super's eyes lit up.

"Her, I know of. Apartment 115. Ground floor. Quiet lady, but nice. Always had a kind word when she saw me. She passed a few years back. Figured the estate would sell the apartment, but it never happened."

"Mind if I take a look in the apartment?"

"You don't think that Fisher guy has been here?"

"I would like to rule out the possibility."

"I've got no problem with that."

"I appreciate your cooperation."

"Come on then. Just—"

"Tony!" someone shouted.

He turned and saw Zach running toward him, Eddie, his beagle, loping beside him.

"Hey, bro. What are you doing here?" he asked as Zach stopped beside him.

"Noah got a call from the precinct. A taxi driver says he remembers picking Martin up from a bus stop last night. He dropped him off two blocks from here. I figured you might need some backup."

"You cleared it with Noah?"

"Don't I always?"

"Probably not."

Zach grinned. "You may be right, but this time I did. I'm not going to do anything that might jeopardize the case against Martin."

"You two coming in or staying out?" the super asked, spitting a wad of gum into the bushes beside the property. "Because I don't want to wait here all day while you chat about life."

He walked into the building.

Tony and Zach followed.

As apartment lobbies went, this was a nice one. Marble floors. Neutral paint. Modern paintings of the New York skyline decorating the walls, but it felt like what it was—an art deco-style apartment complex built nearly a century ago.

"Do you have security cameras?" Zach asked as the super led them through the lobby and into a well-lit hall.

"Nah. We haven't had problems. Like I said, most of the residents are older. Quiet. They do their thing and leave each other alone. The apartment you want is down here. End of the hall."

He stopped at apartment 115, knocked and then unlocked the door.

It swung inward, revealing a small living area. A couch covered in floral-patterned fabric sat against a wall. Dark wood end tables flanked it.

"Place looks like it's been cleaned recently," the super said, running his finger over the coffee table. "Came in and checked on the unit a few weeks ago, and there was a layer of dust on everything. Thought it was a shame. What with how hot a commodity apartments in the area are. Maybe the family is finally going to put it on the market. Go on and do what you need to. I've got a faucet leaking in another apartment that isn't gonna fix itself. You need anything, you'll find me there. If you don't need anything, just close the door when you leave. It'll lock automatically." He walked into the hall, hands shoved in his pockets, bald head gleaming in the overhead light.

"What do you think?" Zach asked as he and Eddie moved through the room. The beagle's tail was wagging, his head down as he sniffed the old Turkish carpet that nearly covered the living room floor.

"I think he's been here," Tony responded. "Rusty led me to one of the windows on this side of the building. It's a nice building, but—"

"Security isn't great?" Zach scratched the beagle behind the ears and walked into a kitchen that opened off the living room. Granite counters, white cabinets and stainless-steel appliances made the small space seem larger. There were no dishes in the sink. No dish soap. Nothing to indicate Martin had been spending time here since his escape.

"Right."

"He's not here now. If he were both our dogs would be going nuts."

"Right." Tony used gloved hands to open a couple of drawers and cupboards. He counted two sets of silverware and two sets of fancy china. A small trash can was tucked beneath the sink. Unlike most of the drawers and cabinets, it was full.

"Look at this," he said, pulling it out and setting it on the floor.

"Anything interesting?" Zach asked, standing beside him as he pulled out a few crumpled receipts.

Tony scanned the first. "Dinner at a café two nights ago."

"So, he has been here."

"Someone has," Tony responded, scanning the next. It was longer and the items on it made his blood run cold.

"What's wrong?"

"Look at this. Baby crib. Diapers. Formula. Baby clothes. Pacifier." He jabbed at the bottom of the receipt. "He purchased this at nine o'clock this morning."

"He knows Katie had the baby," Zach growled, his eyes dark with worry and anger.

"And, he's bought everything he needs for her arrival." Tony strode down a small hallway, slamming the palm of his hand against a door that was partially open. The room beyond was small and filled with everything necessary to bring a baby home. Crib. Set up and ready. Changing table. Small dresser. Tony checked the drawers. They were filled with clothes and diapers.

He walked into the second bedroom. Like the living room, it was furnished, the bed and dresser dated, the small closet opened to reveal men's clothes hung from wire hangers. A map of Queens and a highlighter lay on the bed. Rusty sniffed both, his hackles raised. He knew the man they had been chasing had been there.

"Tony," Zach called. "What do you make of this?"

He walked into the room, carrying what looked like a set of blue scrubs. "They were hanging in the closet in the other room. Check out the tag."

He did, and his heart stopped as he read the name of the hospital where Katie had had the baby.

He didn't think about what he was doing, didn't have any plan in mind aside from making sure Katie and Jordyn Rose were okay.

"Call Noah. Let him know what we've found," he said, yanking out his cell phone and dialing Katie's number.

It rang three times before she answered, her voice groggy with sleep. "Hello? Tony? Is everything okay?"

"Sure," he lied. "I just wanted to check in. Make sure you and the baby are getting the rest you need."

"We are. Well, I am. Jordyn Rose has been with the nurses for..." She paused, and he could picture her looking at the time on her phone, her silky blond hair falling around her shoulders. "Nearly three hours! Wow! I really did need some sleep."

"You said she's with the nurses?" he asked, his pulse rate jumping as he realized the two weren't together.

"Yes. I was so exhausted, the shift nurse offered to take her to the nurses station and keep her until she needed to be fed. Which should be soon."

He could hear bedcovers shifting as she sat up.

"Why? Is something going on that I need to know about?"

"No," he lied again, and despised himself for it. He

made a habit of speaking the truth, of being a straight shooter who wasn't afraid to say difficult things.

But, he couldn't tell Katie what he and Zach had found. Not without filling her with panic. "Are your in-laws back?"

"No, but they should be soon. Are you sure there's nothing wrong? You sound…worried."

"I *am* worried."

"Tony, please just tell me what's going on," she begged, and he knew he had to. That keeping the information from her wouldn't keep her or the baby safe.

He gave her a brief overview.

When he finished, she was silent.

"Katie," he began.

"I need to make sure she's okay," she replied, and then the call went dead.

# TEN

She didn't bother with shoes.

She didn't put on a robe.

She ran from the room, her head spinning, her pulse racing.

"Ma'am." A police officer grabbed her arm, and she shoved him away.

"Mrs. Jameson," he tried again, following her as she hurried through the corridor. "You need to stay in your room and stay in bed."

"I need to find my baby."

"She's with the nurses. I checked on her twenty-five minutes ago. She was fussing a little, but they were getting her back to sleep."

"You're sure?" She swung around, knowing she looked crazed and wild-eyed, but she didn't care.

He nodded, grabbing her arm again when she swayed with relief.

"You need to get back in bad. You're white as a sheet."

"I want to see my daughter first." Because her mind was running through what he'd said, picking apart his words and finding reason to be concerned. "If she was fussing, she needs to eat. They should have brought her to me already."

"She probably went back to sleep," he said, obviously trying to reassure a woman whom he thought might be on the verge of tears.

And, maybe she was.

Her eyes burned. She felt physically ill, her stomach churning, her head spinning. She pressed her hands to her abdomen, praying this was all a bad dream, that she would wake in a moment with Tony beside her, brushing hair from her cheek and whispering that everything was okay.

"Newborns need to eat every couple of hours. It's been nearly three. She did not go back to sleep. Where is she?" she nearly howled.

"Katie, you need to calm down." A second officer appeared at her side, cupped her shoulders and looked into her eyes. "You're going to pass out if you don't start breathing."

"I am breathing."

"Not enough," the officer said kindly, her eyes rich chocolate, her hair a short Afro beneath her uniform cap.

"Please stop worrying about me and go find Jordyn Rose," she begged, feeling so dizzy, she had to lean against the wall to keep from falling.

"She needs a wheelchair," the first officer said, a note of panic in his voice.

"I need to see my daughter."

"That's not going to happen if you're out cold on

the floor," the second officer said gently. "Calm down, okay? I'm going to get a wheelchair. I'll have the nurse bring Jordyn Rose to you."

She walked away, her confidence easing some of Katie's panic. Of course, Jordyn Rose was with the nurses. Of course, she was okay. The baby had been checked on twenty-five minutes ago. She had been fine then, and she was fine now.

But, the couple of minutes it should have taken the officer to return stretched into five and then ten.

"Something is wrong," Katie said, pushing away from the wall and taking a shaky step in the direction the officer had gone.

"You're still in no condition to take a walk down the hall," the first officer said, trying to pull her to a stop. She met his eyes and saw her own fear reflected there.

"You know it's true. If things were fine, she'd have returned by now."

"It can take a while to find a wheelchair. Even in a hospital. How about we just walk back to your room? It's not that far."

She didn't respond. There was nothing she could have said.

Instead, she took another shaky step and then another.

*Please, God. Please let her be there.*

The prayer ran through her head over and over again, a silent, desperate mantra. When she finally reached the end of the hall, she could see the counter that surrounded the nurses station and the monitors that sat on desks there. A whiteboard with patients' names. Hers was there. And Jordyn Rose's.

She could see the bassinet sitting between two chairs. Empty. The nurses were congregated near one side of the counter, faces pale, eyes wide. The female officer stood with them, holding a radio in her hand, her expression dark. Noah was beside her, and his father and brother Carter were flanking him. Ivy was a few feet away, collapsed on a chair near the waiting room, Violet, Rachelle and Lani hovering around her, their own expressions full of worry.

She was the first to see Katie, and when their eyes met, her face crumbled, tears sliding down her cheeks, a sob escaping some deep, dark place inside.

At the sound, the Jameson men rushed to her side.

Ivy must have said something to them, because all three turned in Katie's direction.

"Katie," Noah began, but whatever he planned to say was drowned out by a voice on the PA system calling for a Code 1 lockdown of the facility.

And, Katie knew, even though the prayer was still running through her head, even though she was telling herself that she was having a nightmare. She *knew* that Jordyn Rose was gone.

Suddenly, Noah was in front of her, trying to pull her into his arms. She stepped back. She didn't want his comfort; she wanted her baby.

"We're going to find her," he said, the words tight with emotion.

She turned and walked away. Stiff. Hollow. Ancient.

She could live to be a thousand and never feel so worn and aged again.

Someone called her name, but she didn't look back and she didn't stop. She walked to her room, stepped inside and closed the door. Her overnight bag was sitting on the floor near the window. She grabbed it and pulled out onesies, diapers and a tiny pair of baby shoes.

The sight made her retch, her empty stomach heaving as she imagined her daughter being held in Martin's murderous hands.

"No," she said, as if that could make it less real and less true. "No."

She took leggings, a T-shirt and a flannel button-down from the bag, not thinking about what she was doing, not thinking beyond that moment.

"Katie?" Noah knocked. She didn't answer.

He could come in or not.

"Katie?" This time, Ivy called through the closed door. "Honey, we're coming in, okay?"

She grabbed her cell phone, ducked into the bathroom and locked the door.

They meant well, but they couldn't give her what she wanted.

They couldn't open the door, hand her the baby and say it had all been a misunderstanding. She knew that just as surely as she knew that if Jordyn Rose were going to be saved, she was the one who would have to do it.

She heard them talking in hushed tones as she changed into her clothes. If she left the bathroom, they would surround her with their love, offering her a million words of comfort that none of them really believed. They would reassure her and plan and explain how they were going to go about rescuing Jordyn Rose, and she would listen to their words and hear the heartbreak beneath them and know that she was responsible for it.

They had lost their son and brother because of Martin's obsession with her.

Now they had lost his daughter.

If not for her, they would still be a family of six.

She couldn't face them. Not yet. And, she wouldn't be able to slip out of the hospital with all of them there. That was her one and only plan: get out of the hospital. She wasn't sure what she would do once she managed to leave. She had no idea where to start searching, but maybe she wouldn't have to. Martin had proved to be extraordinarily gifted at finding his way into her world. All she needed to do was give him an opportunity to kidnap her.

Because wherever he was, that's where Jordyn Rose would be.

Her legs went weak, and she collapsed.

She sat where she was, leaning back against the door and staring at her phone. She willed it to ring the same way she had willed Jordan to be alive the day he had failed to show up at the K-9 graduation ceremony the morning he'd been killed. She had willed him to life, but she had known, even while she hoped it wasn't true, that he was gone.

She didn't feel the same about Jordyn Rose.

Her daughter was alive, because Martin had no reason to kill her. She was the perfect pawn in the game he had been playing—an easy means to control Katie. He had to know that.

So, why hadn't he called?

"Ring," she muttered, her voice shaking, her body numb with terror.

The phone remained silent, and she realized the hospital room had gone silent, too. Had they moved into the hall to discuss things? If they had, was it possible she could sneak past them and make it to the stairwell?

Probably not.

Even if she could, the hospital was on lockdown. If she tried to leave, she would be stopped. She was trapped by the concern of the people around her.

And, her daughter was trapped in the arms of a madman.

"Katie!" Tony called. "I'm coming in."

Something scraped the doorknob. It jiggled and then the lock snapped open.

"Katie?" he repeated, the door bumping her back as he tried to open it.

"Scoot over a little, okay?" he said.

She didn't think she had the power to move, but she found herself sliding sideways until her back was against the cool tile wall. The chill of it made her think of the November air and her tiny baby, wrapped in a thin blanket as she was carried through the streets of New York City.

Her head spun, and she leaned it against the wall, trying to keep herself from spinning away with it.

Tony stepped into the bathroom and closed the door. "I asked everyone to go into the waiting room, to give you some time and space right now. We're all beside ourselves, but we're going to get Jordyn Rose back, Katie. We will."

Katie couldn't speak.

He sank down beside her and pulled her into his arms. She sat stiffly, her body rigid with fear.

"I'm sorry, Katie," he murmured, stroking her hair, his calloused fingers catching in the tangled strands.

She started sobbing.

"Shhhhh. You're going to make yourself sick," Tony said, his lips against her forehead, his hand flat on her back.

Katie couldn't stop crying. The sound that ripped from her throat was filled with every bit of the agony that was in her heart.

"I'm breaking into a million pieces," she sobbed.

"Shhhhh," he repeated, pulling her into his lap and wrapping her in his arms. "I'll hold you together."

She didn't think he could, but her arms slipped around his waist and her head dropped to his chest, the agonizing cries of her broken heart muffled by his shirt.

Tony had known rage before.

He had known fear.

He had even, on a few occasions, known helplessness.

But, nothing compared to the emotions racing through his blood as he held Katie and listened to her cry.

Jordyn Rose was gone, somehow taken right out from under the noses of half a dozen nurses. Noah and Zach were questioning the nursing staff, while Carter tried to comfort his parents, Violet, Rachelle and Lani, assuring them that the K-9 unit would find the baby.

And, Tony was here, trying to hold himself and Katie together.

He smoothed her hair, his hands tangling in the long strands, his mind jumping back to the moment after Jordyn had been laid on her chest. Her joy. Her contentment. Her triumph. In that moment, she had seemed like the strongest woman he had ever met. Now she was broken and defeated; her body had gone limp once her sobs had finally faded.

Martin was responsible for this, and for the first time in his career in law enforcement, Tony understood the rage and grief that drove some people to take the law into their own hands.

"I am going to find him, and I am going to make him pay for this," he muttered, his muscles tight, his jaw tense. He wanted to jump up and rush outside with Rusty. The scent trail was fresh. They couldn't be more than forty minutes behind Martin.

But, Katie was holding on to him as if she were drowning and he were her lifeline.

He couldn't leave her. Not like this.

"I want you to find him, and I want you to get my daughter back," Katie said, her voice shaky, her face pressed against his chest.

"I will," he promised, praying he could do what he said.

She nodded, her warm breath seeping through his shirt as she took a deep, shuddering breath.

Finally, she lifted her head and looked into his eyes. Her face was pale and streaked with tears, but there was fire in her eyes. "He already took my husband. He can't have my baby, too."

"He won't."

"He does, and it's my fault. I never should have—"

"Stop blaming yourself for things you had nothing to do with," he said, wiping the tears from her cheeks, his palms resting there.

"I should have kept her in my room. I should have—"

"Known that Martin could somehow get past several levels of security? You couldn't know. None of us could, so instead of beating ourselves up, let's go out, find her and bring her home."

She nodded solemnly, swiped a few more tears from her cheeks and stood.

"I'm ready," she said, as if she had girded herself for battle and planned to ride into the fray.

"You need to stay here. We're going to have patrol officers escort you home as soon as the doctor clears it. If Martin got into the hospital once, he may be able to do it again."

"If he does, maybe he'll have Jordyn Rose with him."

"Don't even think about sacrificing yourself to free your daughter," he said, worried about the look in her eyes—the stoic determination he read in her face.

"Wouldn't you?"

He didn't answer, because he wouldn't lie.

"That's what I thought." She wrapped her arms around her waist, and he could see the soft curve of her belly where the baby had once been.

Somehow, that hurt almost as much as seeing the grief and fear in her eyes.

"Promise me you'll stay here until the doctor releases you," he said, his hands settling on her shoulders, his fingers resting on the jutting ridges of her scapula.

"Tony…"

"Promise me, Katie. I can't concentrate on finding Jordyn Rose if I'm worried about where you might be or what kind of trouble might be finding you."

"All right. I promise I'll stay here until the doctor releases me. But, remember, I'm counting on you to find Jordyn Rose and bring her back to me." Her voice broke, and he pulled her close, pressing a kiss to her forehead and then her cheek.

Without forethought, without planning, his lips brushed hers. Gently. Barely a touch, but they both froze, staring into each other's eyes, breaths mingling, lips millimeters apart.

It would have taken no effort at all to kiss her again.

Kiss her like he meant it.

Like she was everything he had never realized he wanted and everything he could ever need.

He stepped back, let his hands fall away. "I'll bring her back to you," he said.

She nodded, and he turned away, opened the door and stepped into her room. He expected it to be empty, but the family had returned from the waiting room. Carter and Ivy were sitting beside each other, Rusty lying at their feet. Violet, Rachelle and Lani all looked worried. And, he wasn't surprised that they hadn't stayed away. They were one of the strongest, tightest-knit families he knew. They would stand beside Katie and support her through this. In the midst of their own grief and fear, they would still offer her the comfort she needed.

Ivy stood when she saw Tony. "How is she?"

"About like you'd expect," he responded. "I need to find Martin and get her baby back."

"Tony!" Zach barreled in, Eddie beside him. "The precinct just got a call from the super at the apartment complex we visited. He said he thinks he saw Martin at the back entrance."

"Did he have Jordyn Rose with him?" Katie stepped out of the bathroom, her face paper-white.

"The super wasn't sure. He wasn't absolutely certain it was Martin, but he was suspicious enough to give us a call," Zach said. "You doing okay, sis?" he asked.

"No. Where are my shoes? I'm coming with you." She tried to step past Tony, but he grabbed her hand, pulling her to a stop.

"You promised, Katie."

"That was before Martin was spotted."

"You promised," he repeated, and she pressed her lips together and nodded.

"You're going to let me know, right? If you find them there, you'll call?"

"I will," he agreed, calling Rusty and hooking him to his lead.

He offered Katie what he hoped was a reassuring smile and headed out the door. He was just over the threshold when she called, "Tony!"

He turned, and she tried to smile.

"Be careful, okay? I want you back, too."

"I will be."

"Ready?" he asked, meeting Zach's questioning eyes.

"Sure," Zach responded, his gaze shifting to Katie before he walked out the door.

He didn't ask questions as they jogged through the hospital corridor and barreled down the stairs. There wasn't time. Something that Tony was grateful for. Because he didn't have answers. He had no idea what to call the thing that seemed to be blooming between him and Katie.

He certainly didn't want to call it love.

That would feel like too much of a betrayal of the man he had once called brother.

He scowled, opening the hatchback of his SUV so Rusty could hop in.

He slammed it shut and jumped in the driver's seat, using sirens and lights to navigate afternoon traffic as quickly as possible. It still seemed to take too long. By the time he reached the apartment complex, several other K-9 vehicles and NYC police cruisers were parked there.

He jumped out of his vehicle, freed Rusty and joined the group.

K-9 officer Luke Hathaway motioned him over, his cadaver dog, Bruno, sniffing the ground nearby.

"How's everyone holding up at the hospital?" he asked.

"Not good," he answered honestly.

"Any idea how Martin managed to get the baby? Hospital security is pretty tight."

"We found scrubs at the apartment. Tagged with the name of the hospital where Katie gave birth," Tony responded.

"I made some inquiries about that," Zach cut in. "According to the nursing supervisor, they had to bring in a few temporary hires to fill in for a couple of nurses who were out on maternity and medical leave. One of them was an RN named William Spears. He was placed by a health-services temp agency that works with the hospital a lot."

"I don't think I like where this is heading," Tony said.

"Yeah. I don't much like it, either, but that doesn't change the fact that Spears was scheduled to work today. He showed up with his ID and credentials at his scheduled time. The staff supervisor said he was tall, very muscular and talked a lot about his wife and newborn daughter. She also said he didn't look like the photo we distributed. He had blond hair, a beard and mustache, and blue eyes."

"Hair and eye color can be changed easily. Beards and mustaches can be bought at any costume shop. It was Martin," Tony said, sick with the knowledge of how far ahead the kidnapping had been planned. Martin must have accessed Katie's medical records at the clinic soon after he escaped the mental institution.

"Noah is accessing hospital security footage, but it sounds like it. The nurses had no reason to be suspicious. He had worked a few other shifts and there had never been a problem. As a matter of fact, the other RNs liked him. When Jordyn Rose started fussing, he offered to take her to her mother. He hasn't been seen since.

He used his access card to open the stairwell door five minutes later. Two officers think they saw him walking through the lobby with an empty car seat in hand and a duffel slung over his shoulder. They didn't stop him, because he was wearing scrubs and had an ID."

"This guy needs to be stopped. Today," Luke spat, his dark eyes flashing with anger.

"I think it's best if we don't tell Katie about the duffel bag," Tony responded, his fists clenched, the force of his rage nearly blinding him.

If Jordyn Rose was in the duffel...

"Here's the rest of it," Zach said. "We sent patrol officers to talk to taxi drivers in the queue outside the hospital. One of them gave a ride to a man who had a newborn in a car seat."

"Where did he drop them off?"

"A few miles from here. At a bus stop."

"So, he could definitely have come here," Tony said, his gaze shifting to the apartment building. He could see Martin's apartment windows. That meant Martin could see them.

*If* he was inside.

"What's the plan?" a patrol officer asked, her gaze sharply focused. "You want us to stay or fall back?"

"If he's in there, he could have a newborn with him. We don't want her hurt. Fall back, and we'll see if we can make contact."

"We'll park in the lot behind the building across the street and spread out on foot. If he's in there and manages to escape, I don't want him slipping through our fingers."

She jogged to her cruiser, calling several other patrol officers to follow.

"What do you think?" Zach asked as their cruisers pulled out of the lot. "Is he in there?"

"My opinion?" Finn Gallagher said as he walked over with his yellow Lab, Abernathy. "He is."

"Why do you say that?" Tony asked.

"I think I saw the shade on that back window move." He pointed to the small window that Tony had found unlocked previously.

"That's the window in the kitchen. The door opens into the living room. No clear line of sight from there to the kitchen," Zach said.

"I don't think we're going to need one," Luke responded grimly as another of the apartment windows slid open and Martin appeared.

He had cropped his hair short and lightened it, but he still looked like the same guy Tony had seen at church dozens of times. Only, now he wore a wild grin that made him look like the madman he was.

"Hey! This has been a fun ride, huh?" he called out, his eyes blazing in his tanned face.

"Where is my niece?" Zach shouted, taking a step toward the window, his hand on his firearm.

Tony pulled him back. "Stay cool," he hissed. "He's trying to rile us up. It gives him a thrill."

"It would give me a thrill to see him locked up for the rest of his life," Zach growled.

"That's going to happen, but first we need to make sure the baby is in a safe location."

"Your niece?" Martin crowed. "Is that what you think? She's not Jordan's baby—she's mine."

"Where is she?" Tony demanded, taking a step closer to the building, trying to distract him from the fact that Finn and Luke were taking their dogs around to the front.

"Not here." He laughed coldly. "My daughter deserves better than a place like this."

He could have been lying. It was possible Jordyn Rose was sitting in the car seat, right beside her kidnapper, but Tony had a sinking feeling he was telling the truth.

"Your daughter is a newborn. She needs to be with her mother," he said, hoping to tap into Martin's delusions and use them against him.

"Don't try to play mind games with me, Knight. It won't work, and your friends coming around the front of the apartment won't work, either. I didn't come here with the baby. I came because this has all been a setup. The crib. The changing table. The diapers. I knew one of you would show up here eventually, and I wanted to prove to you, once and for all, that you can't beat me at this. Only I know the rules of the game, because I'm the one who wrote them. Now, back off before things get ugly." He pulled a gun and pointed it straight at Tony's head.

The guy was delusional enough to risk coming here, maybe to pick up some baby supplies. He had to know the entire K-9 unit was searching for him and Jordyn Rose and that this apartment was the first place they'd look. Martin clearly wasn't thinking straight, and that would work in Tony's favor.

Or it would get him killed.

"Put that down, Martin," Tony demanded.

"I don't think so. I think you're going to have to make a choice—let me go or kill me. Of course, if you kill me, your precious Katie won't ever see her baby again."

"Katie isn't mine," he said, keeping his voice calm as he moved closer. Rusty was beside him, pressed against his leg and growling low in his throat. He would attempt to disarm Martin if Tony gave him the command, but there was too much risk involved in that.

"You want her to be, and I don't like that." Martin climbed through the window and stood with the building to his back, his gun still pointed at Tony. "She's mine. I won't let anyone take her from me."

"Don't you think she should have some say in that?" Zach asked.

"If she hadn't been brainwashed by your brother, I might. Step back. Both of you." He wore a backpack that was only partially zipped, a few diapers peeking out of the top of it.

Obviously, his story about coming to the apartment to prove something to the K-9 unit had been a lie. He had taken Jordyn Rose somewhere and realized he didn't have the supplies he needed there. So, he'd risked coming here, even with the kidnapping of the baby already making the news. Martin was definitely not thinking clearly. His delusions were crowding out his ability to plan like the experienced, cold-blooded criminal he was.

"Give yourself up, Martin," Tony said. "You can't get away, and I don't want to have to hurt you."

"You wouldn't dare hurt me. I'm the only one who knows where that little brat is. I left her alone, you know. Without someone to feed her, she'll be dead in a day or two. At most." He spoke with cold precision, his eyes suddenly empty of emotion.

"You call your own baby a brat?" Zach said, moving sideways, so that Martin would have more difficulty keeping them both in his field of vision.

"It's all part of the game, Zach Jameson. I won when I played your brother. Let's see if I win with you." He swung his gun toward Zach, then pressed it against his own head.

"So, here is the deal, boys. I can leave, or I can die. You get to choose. Of course, if you choose me dying, the baby dies, too."

"Back down!" someone shouted from across the street.

Tony didn't shift his focus, but he recognized Noah's voice.

"Good call, Chief," Martin called, sidling past Tony, the gun still pressed to his head.

He might pull the trigger if Tony went for him.

He might not.

But, Tony wouldn't risk Jordyn Rose's life on a fifty-fifty shot. If Martin had come for baby supplies, the baby was still alive.

That was exactly the way Tony wanted things to remain.

He holstered his gun.

"I see you understand the rules now, Knight. Good. Maybe you won't join your buddy in the graveyard. Don't follow me. If I see one cop, I will pull this trigger. I'm not afraid to die."

Dozens of onlookers had gathered and were recording on their cell phones as Martin backed away, the gun pressed to his temple, diapers sticking out of his backpack.

Tony wanted to shout that the onlookers were in a volatile and dangerous situation and they needed to leave, but he didn't want to do anything to send Martin off the deep end.

As long as Jordyn Rose was alive, there was hope of rescuing her.

That had to be the focus and the mission.

Martin reached the street and stepped in front of an oncoming car, waving the gun at the startled driver, who swerved and jumped the curb.

Half a dozen people jumped out of the way, screaming as the car bounced toward them.

Tony ran toward the crowd, stopping when Martin shouted his name. He had already crossed the street and was standing on the corner, the gun pressed to his temple again.

"Give Katie my love when you see her. Tell her we'll be together again soon."

Then, before Tony could respond, Martin shifted the gun, aimed and fired in Tony's direction.

# ELEVEN

Katie had watched the video footage at least ten times.

Each time, she flinched when Martin pulled the trigger.

Each time, she expected to see Tony fall to the ground injured. Or, worse.

Each time, she prayed that someone would grab Martin before he escaped and demand that he bring them to Jordyn Rose.

But, of course, that couldn't happen.

The video had been shot nearly ten hours ago. A bystander had sent it to a local news station, and now the entire nation knew just how delusional and dangerous Martin was. He had taunted Tony with a shot that had slammed into a building nearby. Then, he had raced through a shocked crowd of pedestrians, gun in hand, firing shots at a few people who got in his way. For the safety of the crowd that had gathered and was watching, Tony hadn't fired in return.

And, for the safety of Jordyn Rose.

Until they knew where Martin had left her, they

couldn't risk killing him. He had known that and used it to his advantage, escaping.

Again.

They also knew that Jordyn Rose was missing, the story of her kidnapping running with the photo Tony had taken—Katie staring down at Jordyn Rose, a soft smile on her face.

It flashed up on the television screen as she scrolled through news stations, her eyes dry from too much crying, her stomach empty.

"Hun, you need to stop torturing yourself," Alexander said, gently taking the television remote from her hand. He and Ivy were staying with her in the apartment while the rest of the Jameson men scoured the city with the NYC K-9 Command Unit. Even Carter was out searching with his German shepherd, Frosty. He had dropped his daughter off at his fiancée Rachelle's apartment. She would be caring for Ellie until Martin was apprehended. Lani, Noah's fiancée, a police officer awaiting the transfer she'd requested so she wouldn't be under the command of her husband-to-be, was acting as a helpful liaison between Katie and the NYC K-9 Command Unit, sharing information even when there wasn't much to report. Zach's wife, Violet, was focusing on Katie and Ivy, bringing them tea and assuring them the team was out there, doing everything to find Jordyn Rose.

"I'm not torturing myself—I'm trying to find some clue as to where my daughter is." Katie stood and walked across the room, still a little light-headed and dizzy. Her milk had come in, and she had no baby to feed, so Ivy had bought her a pump. Each time she used it, she cried.

She had cried so much, she had no tears left.

*Please, God, keep her safe*, she prayed as she walked to the window that looked out over the front yard. There were three police cruisers parked there, the officers in them assigned to make certain Martin didn't come for Katie.

She wished he would.

She wished he would find a way in and take her to her daughter.

Anything would be better than waiting for something to happen.

"Sweetheart," Alexander said, clearing his throat and putting an arm around her shoulder. "I never had a daughter, but I always thought it would be nice. I always imagined me and the boys fighting off the young studs who wanted to date her."

"You would have done that for certain," she said hollowly, her gaze focused on the street and the houses beyond it. Martin was smart. Would he attempt to get to her with so many guards around?

"What I'm trying to say is that I love you like the daughter I never had. I hate to see you like this, drawn and scared. Not eating. Jordyn Rose is going to need you healthy when she comes home. If you're sick, how will you care for her?"

"I can't eat until I know she has," she said, because just thinking about food made her stomach churn.

"I understand, sweetheart," Ivy said. She was in the kitchen with Violet, stirring something that smelled like beef broth. "No mother wants to eat if she thinks her child hasn't. But, Martin Fisher is delusional. He is not dumb. He knows he can't have you without Jordyn Rose. If he…doesn't take good care of her, he'll have nothing to bargain with."

"I hope you're right," she said. Her heart thudded in her ears, the sound nearly drowning out the soft conversation that drifted up from the yard below. Two of the officers were chatting, their voices light and easy.

She didn't want to resent them for that.

They were doing everything they could to protect her, and she couldn't blame them for her sorrows.

But, she wanted a little less sadness and a little more joy. She wanted to recapture that moment when she had looked at her daughter's face and felt as if everything in her life was working out just right.

More than anything, she wanted her daughter in her arms.

She wanted safety, security and the sense of peace that came with those things.

"I made bone broth, Katie." Ivy cut into her thoughts. "I know you're not keen on eating, but all you have to do is sip. It's rich and filled with iron. Something you need if you're going to produce enough milk for your daughter."

"I can't, Ivy," she said. Just the thought of sipping something made her gag.

"Try," Alexander said, the warmth of his tone and the sadness in his voice reminding her that she wasn't the only one scared and grieving.

"Okay. I'll try."

"And, how about we turn off the television and listen to some music? I always find that to be soothing." He took the remote and turned off the news just as another photo of Katie and Jordyn Rose flashed across the screen.

"Okay," she agreed, because her in-laws were doing everything they could to stay strong for her, and she needed to do the same for them. Quiet music filled the room, and Katie settled in the recliner and closed her eyes, letting the soft strains of an old hymn wash over her. God knew. He understood. He was in control.

She needed to remember that.

"Here, sweetie." Ivy pressed a mug of hot broth into her hands. "Just take little sips. You don't want to upset your stomach." There were shadows beneath her eyes and worry lines near her mouth. Katie imagined that, if her mother had lived, she would have looked the same.

"You have some, too, Ivy," she said. "Sit down and rest for a while. It's not like any of us have anywhere to go."

Ivy smiled tiredly. "You're right about that, and this has been a very long and exhausting day."

"Sit down, Ivy," Violet said gently. "I'll get you some broth. And, how about one of those dinner rolls you brought up from the apartment?"

"Just the broth. Thank you, Violet."

Alexander got up. "I'll help you, Violet. I need something to do." He followed Violet into the kitchen.

Ivy settled onto the couch, watching as Katie took a sip of the broth. "Not bad, right?"

"It's delicious. Thank you, Ivy."

"No thanks necessary. I've always loved to cook. Ellie has just started helping me in the kitchen. In a few years, Jordyn Rose will be doing the same."

Katie nodded, swallowing another sip of broth past the hard lump of fear in her throat.

"It's going to happen. I know it. God isn't going to take Jordyn Rose from us. We already lost her father."

Her voice cracked, and Katie set the mug on the side table and reached to touch her arm. "Ivy, it's going to be okay."

"Aren't I the one who is usually saying that to you?"

"We all have the ability to be strong when we need to be. You've been strong for me dozens of times these past few months. Now, it's my turn to be strong for you."

"You're a wonderful young woman, Katie. I was so happy when you and Jordan married. I didn't think there would ever be a woman who could capture his heart enough to tug him away from his work."

She hadn't. Not really. Jordan had loved Katie enough to marry her, but he had been devoted to his job in a way that had not left room for much else. She felt disloyal thinking that. Jordan was gone. His life had been cut short. She wanted to celebrate the love they had shared rather than dwell on the things they hadn't.

"Your family has been a blessing to me. I don't know what I would have done without you these last few months."

"You would have been just fine."

"Maybe, but I'm glad I didn't have to find out," she said, taking another sip of broth because she didn't want Ivy to see the tears in her eyes.

The Jamesons had taught her valuable lessons about family and loyalty and faith. And, no matter what Ivy said, she really didn't think she could have made it through the last nine months without them.

"Tony has been a tremendous help to you, as well," Ivy said as Violet handed her a bowl of broth. "Thank you, dear," she said to Violet.

Katie smiled at Violet, then turned back to their mother-in-law. "Yes. He has."

"He's a wonderful person. Warm. Caring. Loyal. All the things a young—"

"Ivy, now isn't the time," Alexander interrupted, coming into the kitchen, carrying a small plate with two buttered rolls on it.

"What?" Ivy responded. "I'm simply pointing out some of the good things in our lives to distract us from thinking about the bad."

"I don't think anything could distract me from thinking about the fact that Jordyn Rose has been kidnapped," Katie said, taking her still-full cup to the sink and rinsing it out. "I think I'll go lie down. If you two don't mind?"

"Of course not. We'll be here if you need anything."

She nodded, bending to kiss Ivy's cheek. "You two should get some sleep, too."

"We will," Alexander assured her. He seemed relieved that she was going to her room. She couldn't blame him. She probably seemed ready to shatter.

She *was* ready to shatter.

Again.

Only, this time, she wouldn't let herself. As horrible

as the situation was, as terrified as she felt, she had to come up with a plan to get her daughter back.

She went into the kitchen to thank Violet and give her a hug. Violet's cell rang—Rachelle checking in on how Katie was doing. Violet squeezed Katie's hand and assured Rachelle that Katie was holding up.

*Barely*, Katie thought as she finally went into her room.

Her cell phone rang, and she closed the door quickly, hoping it was Martin. Praying it was him.

"Katie?" Tony said, his voice nearly drowned out by the sound of traffic rushing by.

"Are you guys still outside?" she asked, glancing at the window and the icy rain that had begun to fall a few hours ago.

"I am standing outside of Griffin's Diner. You know the place?"

"Yes. Jordan took me there a few times when we were dating. He said it was the place to hang out if you were part of the K-9 Command Unit. I heard it was closing this month."

"Next week. The owner, Lou, called the precinct to let us know he was staying open late during our search so we could stop in and warm up."

"That was nice of him."

"He's a nice guy, but that's not why I called. I wanted to check in and see how you were doing."

"I'm okay."

"I wish I believed that."

"I'm not okay," she corrected. "But, I'm not going to break down again."

"There isn't anyone who would judge you if you did," he said, his gentle tone reminding her of the way it had felt to be wrapped in his arms, to have his lips brush her forehead and cheek and mouth.

For the first time in as long as she could remember, she had felt like she was home.

"I'm not worried about being judged," she said, her voice raspy and her throat raw from all of the tears she had shed. "I'm worried about being strong enough to get my daughter back. Breaking down isn't going to help me do that."

He was silent long enough for her to know he was choosing his next words carefully. "Katie, I know it's difficult to sit and do nothing when someone you love is missing—"

"You didn't sit and do nothing when Jordan was missing. And, you're not sitting and doing nothing now," she pointed out. "You're a police officer. Even when you are off duty, you know the system and you can use it to your advantage. All I can do is pray and watch countless replays of you facing off with Martin."

"Prayer is a lot."

"I know, but I still feel like I should be doing something more."

"You staying here and staying safe is the best thing you can do for your daughter," he responded.

"What if…?" She couldn't bring herself to ask, but Tony seemed to hear the unspoken question.

"Jordyn Rose is alive," he said.

"We can't know that, and that's what is eating at me. That's what scares me more than anything," she admitted, her eyes hot and dry, her heart skipping beats. She felt dizzy and sick; the thought of her tiny baby dead at the hands of Martin Fisher nearly stole her breath.

"She is, Katie."

"How can you know?"

"He had diapers in his backpack, for one."

"And, for two?"

"He knows he will never get his hands on you if he doesn't have the baby with him."

"That's what Ivy said."

"We can't both be wrong, can we?" he asked, and she knew he was trying to make her smile. Even now, when he was exhausted and frustrated and working every angle possible to try to find Jordyn Rose, he cared enough about her to do that.

"Yes, but I'm hoping you aren't. I am hoping that, this time, things will have a happy ending."

"We're doing everything we can to make sure that happens, and that is why I called. Don't go maverick on me, okay?"

"What do you mean?" But, of course, she knew.

He had to understand how desperate she was, how willing to do anything to get Jordyn Rose back.

"If he calls you, I want to know it. And, if he tries to get you to leave the house, stay put. We'll trace the call and track him down. He can't move fast with a baby in his arms."

"He didn't have a baby when he nearly shot you," she said, the image of Tony diving sideways as the bullet slammed into the brick building behind him filling her head.

"That was before all the publicity. He can't leave her where someone can hear her crying. He can't ask someone to watch her, and he can't waste time. The entire city is hunting for him. He's going to contact you, Katie. And, when he does, I want you to call me immediately."

"I will," she agreed.

"Good. I've got to go. We're going to regroup and head out to search again."

"Be careful, Tony."

"I will," he said before he disconnected.

She set the phone on the bedside table, flicked off the overhead light and lay down. Ice pattered against the windows, and the hushed whisper of leaves brushing against the side of the house reminded Katie of the first winter she had spent there with Jordan.

If she had known it would be the last, she wouldn't have worried so much about the time he spent away, she wouldn't have resented his distracted attitude. Maybe she would have dwelled in the beauty of each moment rather than in the disappointments.

"If I could do it again, I would be more grateful," she whispered, and she knew if Jordan had been there, he would have told her it was okay. He would have reminded her, as he often had, that no one was perfect. That they were all fallible human beings.

He would have been right, but that didn't make her feel any better about things. Jordan was gone, and any chance she had to appreciate every part of their marriage was gone. She wouldn't spend her life mourning that, but she wasn't ever going to make the same mistake again.

If she got Jordyn Rose back—*when* she did—she would remind herself every morning that the day was a gift to be used and appreciated. Every night she would thank God for the good, the bad and every single moment in between.

"Please, Lord," she whispered. "Let me have my baby back. Please."

She wanted an audible answer, some sign that everything really would be okay. Instead, she felt nothing but the ache in her abdomen where Jordyn Rose had once been.

The floorboards outside the room creaked as Ivy and Alexander made their way through the apartment. She listened as the door closed and the bolt slid home. Minutes later, water ran through the pipes in the walls. She could imagine them in their apartment, making another pot of coffee as they discussed all the things they hadn't dared say when she was nearby.

They had embraced her like one of their own, and she would never forget that.

The apartment went quiet, the old house sighing as it settled for the night. Minutes passed and then an hour, and Katie was still wide-awake.

When her phone rang, she jerked upright and grabbed it without looking at the caller ID. "Hello?" she said, and then realized that the phone was still ringing.

Surprised, she scrambled out of bed, following the sound to the overnight bag she had brought to the hospital. She set it near the closet but hadn't unpacked it yet. The ringing stopped, then began again as she unzipped the bag, dug through the clothes and pulled out a flip phone. Not hers, but ringing.

She answered, her voice shaking. "Hello?"

"Finally, my love. You found the phone I left for you. Our daughter and I have missed you," Martin said, the sweet cooing sound of his voice making her skin crawl. Had he accessed her bag at the hospital? Or had he somehow slipped into the apartment before she had the baby and put the phone there then?

"Is she all right?" she asked, unable to keep the desperation from her voice.

"Don't you trust me to be a good father to our child?" he responded, the hard edge in his tone alarming her more than his sweet talk had.

"Of course, I do. It's just… I was nursing her in the hospital, and it's been hours since she has eaten."

"No worries, darling. I researched everything when I was planning our escape. I got Alison the best baby formula, and she has been eating every three hours."

"Alison?"

"It was my grandmother's name. Do you like it?"

"It's beautiful," she responded, because she needed to become part of his delusion if she was ever going to see Jordyn Rose again.

"I'm glad you think so. If you didn't, I might consider another option. Although, it is the man's right to make the decisions in the family. Don't you agree?"

"Yes, of course," she lied.

"Have you missed me?"

"I've been waiting for your call," she responded, sidestepping the question because she couldn't make herself say that she had.

"I'm sorry if you were worried, my love. I had to

wait until I was sure your guards were asleep. I saw their lights go out a while ago, but you can never tell with people like that."

"Where are you?" she asked, running to the window and staring out into the darkness, hoping she might see him standing there with her baby.

"Not as close as I was. Now, listen carefully. I'm only going to say this once." The steel edge was back in his tone, and she tensed, waiting for instructions and hoping she didn't forget them.

"Are you familiar with the Queensboro Bridge?"

"Yes." It was seven or eight miles away and spanned the East River from Long Island City to the Upper East Side in Manhattan.

"Good. We don't have a lot of time. The city is crawling with police. But, we can do anything together. Even escape them. I hired an Uber to pick you up three blocks from your apartment. That little coffee shop where you and Jordan had your first date."

"How do you know about that?"

"I know everything about you. Now, stop asking questions and listen! The Uber is already waiting. If you're not there in ten minutes, something terrible might happen to our daughter."

"There are three police officers outside. How am I supposed to get past them?"

"You're smart. I have no doubt you'll figure it out. I left a prepaid cell phone under a rosebush at the east corner of the parking lot. Make sure you pick it up before you get in the Uber. My contact information is already programmed in. I want you to call me as soon as the Uber leaves."

"I will," she said.

"Good. You'll be dropped off a few blocks away from the bridge. Use the pedestrian walkway and meet me on the Manhattan side. Leave your cell phone at the apartment. If you have it when you get here, it won't be a very nice trip to our new home."

He disconnected, and she looked around the room, frantically trying to find something that would help her get past the police. She thought about telling them the truth, but she was afraid Martin might still be watching. If he saw her talking to them, he might make good on his threat to harm the baby.

She eased the door open and slipped through the hallway. She didn't dare grab her jacket from the closet, but she had left her shoes near the front door and she slid into them. She glanced out the front window and could see the police officers sitting in their cars, engines idling as they waited for something to happen. She didn't think she could get out the front door without being noticed.

She still had the flip phone in hand, and it buzzed as she switched directions and headed toward the back door and the deck. She glanced at the text message that had come through, her heart nearly stopping when she saw a selfie of Martin holding Jordyn Rose close to his face.

Hurry, my love. We're waiting.

She was terrified of running out of time, but she was just as worried about leaving without letting Tony know where she was headed. She ran back to her room and grabbed her cell phone. She didn't have time to do anything more than that. She was afraid any hesitation on her part, any slow progress on doing what Martin had demanded, and he might harm the baby. She tucked the cell phone in her pocket, shoved the flip phone in with it and eased the back door open. She was breathless and light-headed. She needed to rest, but the clock was ticking and the car was waiting. If she missed it, she would have to find another way to get to the bridge.

She managed to get out the door and down the stairs without being noticed. She headed across the yard and climbed the fence, dropping onto the neighbor's property.

Then, with a quick prayer for protection, she darted through the yard and raced away.

Tony followed Rusty through the lower level of the apartment complex. Noah's fiancée, Officer Lani Branson, was there to help strategize, even though she wouldn't be working the case on the street with a K-9 partner. Lani's request for a transfer hadn't come through yet, but soon she'd be working with another K-9 unit in one of the five boroughs. Last month, Lani had helped capture Martin, her long blond hair and blue eyes giving her enough of a resemblance to Katie to draw Martin's attention.

As far as everyone in the K-9 unit was concerned, Lani had proved her merit when she had gone face-to-face with the man who had murdered their chief. The team was sorry to lose her but understood why she requested a transfer.

"Rusty doesn't seem interested in much here," Lani said as she and Tony walked through lower level of the apartment complex for the second time. They had returned there, hoping that Martin might have done the same.

"We know Martin was here before. I was hoping he came back, and Rusty might be able to catch his scent."

"We're going to find him. You know that, right? He can't stay hidden forever."

"Maybe not, but he's managed to do it for almost eight months."

"He can't do it forever," she repeated. "We're going to find him, and we're going to get Jordyn Rose back."

He glanced at Lani, grateful she was here as a kind of liaison between the police and the Jameson family. "I know," he said.

She nodded, her expression grim but determined.

He walked outside, disappointed that Rusty hadn't found a scent trail to follow but not ready to give up. Martin had been in the area. They knew that. Rusty was a fantastic search-and-rescue dog, and he had scent-tracked Martin enough to know he was looking for someone specific.

"Want to give it another go, Rusty?" Tony asked.

Rusty whined in response.

They crossed ice-coated grass, Tony ignoring the hail that fell on his head and shoulders. Rusty trotted beside him, head up, tail alert. He loved his job and the game it represented to him. He also loved the tug toy reward he got for a job well-done.

"Ready, boy?" Tony asked, and the Lab strained against his hold. "Find!"

Rusty darted toward the street, his lighted collar glowing orange against his dark fur. An old residential area of Queens, this neighborhood was quiet after dark. Cars lined both sides of the street, bumper-to-bumper, and gleamed in the darkness. Rusty nosed the ground near the curb, rounding one of the vehicles and then returning. He huffed deeply, stacking scents as he continued to try to locate the trail.

Trained in both urban and wilderness air scent, Rusty was one of the best in the country. When he returned to Tony's side and began the process again, it was obvious he hadn't been able to find a scent trail.

"Nothing?" Noah asked, striding toward him, Scotty beside him.

"I'm afraid not."

"Same for every other team that tried." Noah brushed ice from his hair and glanced at the house. "Is Lani still inside?"

He nodded. "I had a rookie call for the evidence team. We found the baby's hospital identification tags in the trash."

Noah shook his head. "I have a bad feeling about this. It's all too well planned."

"I agree."

"Have you been in contact with Katie?"

"I spoke to her while we were at Griffin's."

"How's she holding up?"

"About as well as can be expected. I was hoping to have some good news for her after we cleared the apartment complex."

"I'm sorry we don't."

"Yeah. I'm sure we all are." He called Rusty back to heel, frowning as his cell phone buzzed. He glanced at the text message that he had received, his heart skipping a beat when he realized it was from Katie:

At Queensboro Bridge. Meeting Martin. Can't talk. Please hurry.

His pulse raced, his hand shaking as he swung around and darted toward his car.

"Something wrong?" Noah asked, jogging after him.

"Katie's gone to meet Martin at the Queensboro Bridge."

"What?"

Tony handed him the cell phone, jogged to his SUV and opened the hatchback for Rusty while Noah read the message.

"You're not planning to rush off alone without a plan, are you?" Noah demanded.

"I'm planning to stop him before he kills someone else I care about."

Tony closed the hatch, took his phone and rounded the vehicle.

"We need to come up with an actual plan before we move in." Noah grabbed his arm and pulled him to a stop.

"Did you see the time stamp on the message? She

sent it fifteen minutes ago. If we don't get moving, we may be too late. Let me go ahead with Rusty. That way if they leave the bridge, I can follow."

Noah hesitated, then nodded. "I'll agree to that if you agree to this—you're not going to let your heart get in the way of your head."

"When have I ever done that?"

"When have you ever cared for a woman the way you care about Katie?"

"This isn't just about Katie," he replied, opening the driver's door and climbing in the SUV. This wasn't a conversation he wanted to have with Jordan's brother. Not now, when there was so much riding on his getting to the bridge before Martin made his escape again.

"No. It's not, but you know what I'm saying." Noah put his hand on the door to keep Tony from closing it.

When Tony didn't respond, he sighed.

"Look, this isn't the time or the place, but for the record, whatever might happen between you and Katie, Jordan would be happy for it. If he can't be here to take care of her and their daughter, he would want you to be the one to do it." He closed the door, patted the hood and walked away.

Tony pulled away from the curb, keeping his speed at a reasonable pace, the icy conditions preventing him from flooring it. He refused to dwell on Noah's words. He refused to think about how obvious his affection for Katie must be.

He hadn't had any intention of falling for his best friend's widow, but somehow, it had happened. No matter how many times he tried to tell himself the feelings were nothing but a product of heightened fear and stress, he couldn't ignore the truth. He had had a soft spot for Katie from the moment he had met her. Now, that soft spot was becoming something more.

He frowned, parking the SUV two blocks from the bridge. The sleet had changed to rain, and he pulled up his hood as he got Rusty out of the back and took off his lighted collar.

There was no sense in announcing their presence before it was necessary.

His phone buzzed as he headed toward the bridge. He checked it quickly, skimming a text Noah had sent. The team was splitting. Half heading for the Queens side of the bridge. Half for the Manhattan side. Patrol officers were joining them, and they'd create barricades to prevent Martin from escaping in a vehicle.

If he showed up.

Tony had a feeling he would.

The guy had one goal and one obsession—Katie. He wouldn't leave New York City without her.

And, Tony?

He had no intention of letting Martin leave at all.

# TWELVE

Katie had never used the Queensboro pedestrian walk-way. If she had, she certainly wouldn't have done it at night. She preferred bright daylight hours to darkness, and if she did venture out at night, she usually didn't do it alone. Now, though, with Jordyn Rose's life at stake, she was willing to do anything she needed to save her daughter.

She approached the bridge cautiously, the rain drench-ing her clothes and shoes. She had been outside for too long, and she was cold to the bone, her teeth chattering as she entered the walkway. She'd left her cell phone tucked under the seat of the car, and she could only hope Tony had gotten her message and was on the way.

Otherwise, she was on her own.

About to face the man who had murdered her hus-band and kidnapped her daughter.

The old steel beams were slick with water, and the wire fencing between the river and the walkway was gray blue in the dim lights. Across the inky water of the East River, Manhattan's skyline beckoned through a hazy fog of frozen air. On any other night, Katie would have thought it was beautiful.

Tonight, it just seemed eerie and sinister.

Several cars passed to her left, and she wondered if a motorist would hear if she called for help. She doubted it. Even if a driver did hear, would he offer help?

She had come because she'd had no choice, but she was terrified, the thought of coming face-to-face with Martin filling her with cold dread. How many times had she seen him at church after Jordan's death? How many times had he told her how sorry he was for her loss? He had even invited her for coffee once or twice, extending the invitation as if he thought company might help ease her broken heart.

She had not realized that he had been the reason for her heartache. She had had no idea that he had created a shrine devoted to her, that from the moment they'd met, he had believed she was God's gift to him.

She shuddered, and the wild baying of a dog sent her pulse racing. It sounded like Reed's bloodhound, Jessie.

Had Tony received her text?

Were members of the K-9 unit hidden nearby, waiting for Martin to show himself.

*Please let that be the case, Lord*, she prayed silently.

Her foot slipped on slick pavement, and she fell, her hand banging into cold metal, the sound reverberating through the walkway.

"Careful, my love. If you damage your hand, the ring I bought you might not fit," Martin whispered, his voice seeming to come from behind her and in front of her.

She swung around, thought she saw something in the shadows at the end of the walkway.

"Where are you?" she called, her voice shaky with fear and adrenaline.

"Right here, my love." He grabbed her from behind, his arm snaking around her waist so unexpectedly, she screamed.

He slapped his hand over her mouth, grinding her teeth against her lips. "Shhhhh. None of that," he said gently.

There was nothing gentle about his touch as he dragged her backward, his hand still over her mouth.

When he finally stopped, they were standing in the shadows of a support beam, sheltered from the rain by a metal overhang.

"Are you going to scream?" he asked, his lips tickling her ear.

She wanted to bite, claw, kick, free herself, but he had both of his hands on her, and that meant he didn't have Jordyn Rose.

She nodded, and he nuzzled her neck. "Good girl," he said, his hands dropping away.

She spun around, ready to beg for her daughter.

A car seat sat near the edge of the bridge, the cover pulled up so that she couldn't see if Jordyn Rose was inside it.

"Is she there?" she breathed, darting toward it.

He yanked her back, slamming her against the support beam. Her head hit metal, and she saw stars.

"Ask permission before you touch our daughter," he growled, shaking her hard enough to make her teeth knock together.

"May I see her?" she begged, desperate to lift the cover and see if her daughter was there.

"I don't see why not. Now that we're finally a family, we should all spend as much time as we can together," he said jovially, as if he had not just slammed her into a metal beam and violently shaken her.

"Thank you, Martin," she said, feeling dizzy, weak and agonizingly hopeful. Jordyn Rose might be less than four feet away, hidden behind the cloth cover that was zipped shut over the car seat.

"Call me darling. I always thought that would be a good pet name," he responded, his eyes hot with fanatical glee.

"Darling," she repeated, sidling past him and moving toward the car seat. More slowly this time, because she was afraid that he would yank her back again, that this was simply a game he was playing for his own amusement and at the end of every round, Katie's arms would still be empty.

She reached the car seat, her hand trembling as she touched the zipper.

*Please*, she prayed. *Please.*

She unzipped it and pulled back the cover. Her head was buzzing as she saw chubby cheeks, a rosebud mouth and a thatch of light brown hair. "Jordyn Rose," she whispered, touching the baby's cheek.

"Alison," Martin snarled, suddenly towering over her.

"I'm sorry. Alison."

"Don't forget again."

"I won't. Can I take her out?" she asked, already reaching for the buckle.

"I guess so. It'll be easier to carry the seat without her deadweight in it."

Katie unhooked the baby quickly, worried he would change his mind.

Jordyn Rose opened her eyes as Katie lifted her from the seat, her rosebud mouth sucking greedily at the air.

"She's hungry," she said.

"I didn't have time to feed her."

"Can I—"

"In the car. If you cooperate."

"Car?"

"I parked on the other side of the bridge. I figured we would be less likely to be found there."

"You're probably right," she said, holding Jordyn Rose close to her chest as he grabbed her arm and started yanking her across the bridge.

Something scuffled on the pavement behind them.

She glanced at Martin, wondering if he had heard.

He seemed focused on the direction they were going. Once they reached the other side of the bridge and got in his car, there would be less of a chance to make an escape. She was certain she had seen something moving at the Queens end of the bridge. She pretended to trip, glancing back as Martin yanked her upright.

"Be careful! We don't have time for your clumsiness."

"Sorry," she said, but she had seen what she needed to—a K-9 officer and his dog creeping through the shadows behind them.

Tony and Rusty. She was certain of it.

"Darling," she said, forcing her voice to be light and flirtatious.

"What?" he snapped.

"I was thinking about our new life. The one you've planned for us."

"Yeah?" He was walking faster, perhaps feeling the net closing in on him.

"Wouldn't it be nicer if it were just the two of us?"

"What do you mean?" He stopped, obviously surprised by her comment.

"The baby." She looked down at her daughter, praying she was doing the right thing.

"What about her? Come on. Speak. We don't have all night for this conversation."

"Let's leave her here. Someone will find her and give her a good home."

His eyes widened, and he dropped her arm.

"What kind of game are you playing?"

"This is no game. I…love you and want to be with you, but Jordan's family will never let us be together if we have his daughter with us."

"You're right," he said, the feverish gleam in his eyes letting her know she had said exactly the right thing.

"Good. Wonderful. Let's put her in the car seat. She'll be fine until morning, when the foot traffic picks up."

"Good idea." He set the seat down, and she strapped Jordyn Rose into it.

She kissed her downy head, zipping the cover back in place as the baby began to whimper.

"Come on, my love," Martin said, taking her hand and pulling her away. "Our chariot awaits."

"Wonderful," she responded, her mouth dry with regret, her pulse racing.

She glanced back one more time.

To say goodbye, and to make certain she had zipped the cover completely.

Tony stepped out of the shadows, easing toward the car seat and lifting it carefully. Seconds later, he was heading back toward Queens, jogging through the rain and fog, disappearing from sight.

The baby was safe.

That was what she had wanted.

It was what had mattered most, but she wanted to be running beside Tony, his arm around her shoulders as they raced to safety.

"What are you looking at?" Martin snapped, spinning her around so she was standing in front of him.

"Nothing," she said, forcing herself to smile at him. "Only you, Martin, my love."

"Liar," he shouted, glancing back and seeing that the car seat was gone.

"Betrayer!" He backhanded her, and she flew backward, landing on hard pavement, the breath driven from her lungs.

"Get up!" he shouted. "Get up and take your punishment."

He had grabbed her by the shoulder and was pulling her upright when lights flashed at both ends of the bridge, the pulsing strobe of emergency vehicles piercing the fog and darkness.

Help had arrived, but she was afraid it was too late.

Martin pulled a gun from beneath his jacket and

pressed it against her jaw, dragging her backward against his chest.

"March," he said, moving across the bridge and forcing her to do the same.

She went without fighting.

The baby was safe.

She prayed that she would be, too.

She wanted the life she had been given. All of it. The triumphs and the sorrows. She wanted to live in the joy of knowing that she had been loved by a wonderful man, that she had begun a family with him and that everything she had dreamed of when she had asked God for a family had come true the day she met Jordan.

Maybe the happily-ever-after wasn't what she had expected, but that didn't mean it couldn't be a good one.

If she survived, she wouldn't be afraid of the future. She would walk into it with an open heart, ready for whatever God brought her way.

Maybe even ready for a new love.

The thought settled in her heart, driving away some of her fear as Martin dragged her closer to the end of the bridge.

Tony had his gun trained on Martin, but he didn't dare pull the trigger. Not with Katie there. He had brought Jordyn Rose to an officer waiting near the end of the bridge and returned as quickly as he could.

It hadn't seemed to be quickly enough.

He had wanted to carry both Katie and the baby away from Martin, make sure they were safe and then return to arrest the man who had murdered his best friend.

"Let her go, Martin," he called.

Martin swung around, the gun slipping from Katie's jaw and pointing in Tony's direction.

"I will kill you, Knight. Just like I killed your friend, and I won't have one moment of regret over it. Back off."

"Maybe you will, but by the time you fire the first shot, half a dozen officers will be storming the bridge. They aren't going to kill you. That would make your life too easy. They're going to arrest you and make sure you never see the light of day again."

"That will never happen," Martin snarled, his gaze darting from Tony to the end of the bridge, where half a dozen emergency vehicles had blocked the entrance to the bridge.

"You're trapped. We have officers and dogs on both sides of the bridge. There is no escape, Martin. It's time to face up to what you've done."

"What I've done? What *I've* done!" he shouted, shoving the gun against Katie's temple. "*You* did this! You and your K-9 buddies. You should have accepted Jordan's death as a suicide. If you had, Katie and I would be together, and none of this would have happened."

"Jordan would still be dead," he reminded him, his focus on Katie.

Strands of wet hair fell over her pale skin, and her clothes clung to her. She was shaking with cold and fear, but she was obviously thinking clearly. Getting the baby out of the line of fire had been genius. He planned to tell her that. Just like he planned to tell her how worried he had been, how much he'd thought about her and the baby as he'd driven to the bridge.

He may not have intended to fall for her, but he knew Noah was right—Jordan would have been happy for him. He would have been pleased to know his best friend would always be there for the woman he had loved.

"Jordan deserved to die for what he did to me. You don't take a man's woman. You don't steal another person's property." His voice grew louder with every word, his eyes wilder, the gun swinging away from Katie. Martin seemed too out of control to notice.

Katie met Tony's gaze, and he thought she was trying to send a silent message. Before he could figure out what it was, she slammed her elbow into Martin's stomach, twisted out of his grip and dodged to the left.

Martin fired, and the shot ricocheted off a metal beam, sending sparks flying.

Katie stumbled, fell to the ground and lay still.

"Freeze!" Tony yelled as Martin took aim at her again.

Martin didn't lower the gun, so Tony fired, the bullet striking its target and hitting just below Martin's collarbone.

The gun dropped from Martin's hand, skidded across the bridge and slid beneath the metal fencing.

"Give up, Martin," Tony commanded as Martin stumbled after the gun, "You can't win."

"You don't think so?" he said, blood seeping from his shoulder, his eyes crazed.

"Look around. There are officers coming at you from

both sides." He gestured to the men and dogs racing toward them.

"You don't understand, Knight. I'm not like the rest of you."

"That's obvious. The rest of us don't murder people in cold blood," Tony retorted, his pulse beating frantically, his desire to rush to Katie's side nearly overwhelming him. "Put your hands up. It's over."

"It isn't over until I say it is," Martin replied. "Stand back and watch me fly."

He rushed for the fence and clambered over it so quickly that Tony barely had time to react. By the time he realized what was happening, Martin was tumbling into the water below.

"Did he jump?" Katie asked, easing into a sitting position, her face pale.

"I'm afraid so." There was no way Martin would have survived the jump. As much as Tony had wanted Martin caught, he hadn't had any desire for him to die.

"Where's Jordyn Rose?" she asked, her blue eyes desperate.

"With a police officer. Safe," he assured her as he hurried to her side. So relieved that it was over, he did the only thing that made sense. He kissed her. Not the easy light brush of lips that he had offered before. This was a real kiss. One filled with passion and with promise.

"What was that for?" she asked when he pulled back.

"You. Me. Us."

"I like the sound of that," she said, smiling into his

eyes, all the tension that she had been carrying since Jordan's death gone.

"Do you?"

"Yes. I was thinking, while Martin was dragging me across the bridge, that if I had a chance to keep living, if God got me through this in one piece, I wasn't going to miss out on whatever He had in store."

"No?"

"No. I've been afraid for a long time. Afraid of losing people I love. Afraid of being alone. Afraid of never having all the things I dreamed of when I was a kid."

"What things were those?"

She smiled, her palm resting on his cheek as she looked into his eyes. "All the things I already have. Family. Friends. A beautiful baby." Her lips grazed his. "Possibilities."

"I like the sound of that," he said, and she laughed.

He captured the sound with his lips, kissing her again, knowing that if he spent a hundred years with her, it wouldn't feel like enough.

"I love you, Katie. I want you to know that."

She pulled back, her smile filled with hope and tinged with sadness. "I love you, too. And, I'm so glad you're part of my life. That you'll be part of Jordyn's."

"I hate to break up the party, but we've got some cleaning up to do and some paperwork to file," Noah said, crouching beside them, Scotty near his feet. "Are you two okay?"

"I'm fine," Tony said, getting to his feet and pulling Katie with him. "Are you?" he asked her.

"Better than I've been in a long time."

"Could have fooled me, sis," Zach said, rushing toward them. "I saw you go down and thought that my heart was about to break. From now on, you stay inside, doors locked, shades drawn. If you do leave the house, I plan to Bubble Wrap you and cover you in Kevlar."

"With Martin…gone," Katie said, some of the tension returning to her face, "I don't think that will be necessary."

"The dive team is ready to go in," Noah said solemnly. "If we can recover his body, that will bring some closure to things."

"It will probably make me feel better," Katie admitted, walking to the railing and looking down. "I wish things could have been different."

"I know," he said as he joined her. "I do, too, but this is how they are. This is where it ended, and maybe, it's where it will begin."

She nodded. No smile this time. No laughter. "I think it will," she said.

"Katie?" Lani called, and they both turned as she hurried toward them, Rusty beside her, the car seat in her hands. "Sorry for barging out here like this, but I've been waiting in the SUV with your sweetie and she's starting to squall. I think she might be hungry."

"I think you're right," Katie said, reaching to lift Jordyn Rose from the carrier.

And, Tony was struck again by the picture they made. Mother and daughter. Looking into each other's faces as they began the process of learning about one another.

"You're beautiful," he said, and Katie looked up, startled, it seemed, by his comment.

"I'm a mess," she murmured, her gaze dropping to her daughter. "And, if I don't feed this little one soon, she will be, too."

"You're beautiful," he repeated, and she finally looked into his eyes again.

"You don't have to say that, Tony."

"I'm saying it because I see it. If I live to be a hundred, I will never forget the way you look right now, standing there with your daughter."

"Thank you," she whispered.

"For the truth?"

"For being you. For being here for me. Every time I've needed you."

Jordyn Rose's face scrunched, and she let out an angry squeal.

"I think that may be our signal to end the conversation," Tony said, touching the baby's face and smiling as she rooted toward his fingers. "For now."

"For now," Katie agreed, and then she lifted Jordyn Rose to her shoulder and headed across the bridge.

"Good job, Tony," Carter said, stepping up beside his brothers.

"I don't think I asked for compliments."

"No, but you would have been getting criticism if you had made one tear fall from Katie's eyes. I figured I would be fair and offer you what you had earned."

"The last thing I would ever want to do is make Katie cry. She has shed enough tears for a while," Tony said.

Noah nodded. "Agreed. I also think we have all had too many long days and nights hunting for answers to Jordan's death." He paused as other members of the

NYC K-9 Command Unit moved in. Luke Hathaway and his dog, Bruno. Finn Gallagher and Abernathy. Brianne Hayes and Stella. Reed Branson and Jessie.

They stood together. A team. A family.

"Let's hope the next few months are a little less challenging," Noah continued.

"They will be for me," Carter said, crouching beside his dog and scratching behind his ears.

"What do you mean?" Noah asked.

"I've been waiting for the right time to say this. Now that we're finally able to close Jordan's case." He cleared his throat, and Tony knew he was thinking about the brother he had lost. The friend they had all lost. "I guess now is as good a time as any. The injury I received isn't healing as quickly as I had hoped. My doctor warned me that I may never be able to return to duty full-time."

"Is he sure?" Tony asked, worried for Carter, wondering what he would do if his law-enforcement job were taken away from him.

"No, but I am." Carter stood, his gaze traveling over the group of men and women who had forged strong bonds through adversity. They had worked together, trained together, fought for justice together. The strength and power of that was in the face of every team member as they returned Carter's gaze. "I can't go back full-time. I don't even know if I would want to. Losing Jordan made me realize that there is more to life than work. But, I can't give you guys up. You're too much a part of me. So, I talked to Lou. He's agreed to allow me to buy Griffin's Diner. He'll show me the ropes over the next few months, and then I'll take over operations.

I may not be working with the K-9 Command Unit, but I'll still be sticking my nose in all of your business for many years to come."

For a moment, there was nothing but silence, and then, one by one, the team members began to clap.

"Brother," Tony said, slapping Carter on the back. "It's the very best news I've heard in a long time."

"I agree," Noah said. "Now, how about we save the celebration for after we process the scene. We've got a lot of work to do before we can go back to the office and move on with our lives. Tony, head out. You've worked too many hours the last few days, and I can't afford to pay you any more. We'll meet at the precinct tomorrow, and you can give me your statement and write up your report."

"You sure?" Tony asked, knowing that Noah was giving him an easy out so that he could join Katie and escort her home.

"I am right now, but if you stand there questioning me for much longer, I might change my mind."

"Then, I guess I'd better get moving. See you tomorrow," he called as he took Rusty's leash from Lani and headed back across the bridge.

Cold rain still fell, splattering the pavement and sliding down Tony's cheeks, but Queens was straight ahead, hundreds of lights shining through the icy fog, beckoning him home.

He had never expected to be in this place—where contentment and peace and joy seemed to embody the word *home*. As a kid, he had avoided being in his parents' house. Their violent arguments had tainted the walls and floor and tinged the air with bitterness. To Tony, home had been an elusive dream, a thing that others attained but that he would never have.

Now, though, he finally understood.

Home was peace, it was companionship, it was friendship and community. It was all of the things he had found while working with the K-9 Command Unit. All of the things he had found with the Jameson family. All of the things he had found in his church. And, it was all of the things he had found when he had looked into Katie's eyes, when he had watched her hold her newborn, when he had felt the first stirrings of love in the depth of his heart.

He hadn't expected it.

He hadn't even wanted it.

But, God had led him on a long and winding path to the one thing that had been missing from his life.

"What do you say, Rusty?" he asked as he neared the end of the bridge and the long line of police cruisers waiting there. "Ready to find Katie and Jordyn Rose so we can go home?"

Rusty's ears twitched, his tail swinging wildly. He barked once, tugging at the end of the leash.

"Okay," Tony said, unhooking him. "Find!"

The Lab took off, springing toward the police cruisers, shooting straight as an arrow toward the car where their future waited.

# EPILOGUE

Graduation day came just like it always did with the K-9 Command Unit. Only this one was different—a redo of the graduation that should have taken place ten months ago. Katie had been preparing for a couple weeks. Not for the ceremony itself, but for the memories that would come with it.

It seemed like a lifetime ago since her alarm had gone off, and she had gotten out of bed, queasy with morning sickness, wishing she could stay in bed. She had taken the day off work so that she could be there when Jordan congratulated the team for graduating another successful pool of puppy candidates.

He had already been heading out the door when she had dragged herself out of bed, and when he had kissed her goodbye, she had had no idea it would be for the last time.

Even now, that broke her heart a little.

Even with all of the joy having Jordyn Rose and Tony in her life brought, her eyes burned with tears when she remembered waving goodbye to Jordan as he walked down the steps.

"I still miss you, Jordan," she said, lifting the wedding photo that sat on the end table in the living room. She had thought about moving it after she and Tony had begun dating, but when she had mentioned that to him, he had kissed her tenderly and told her that he had loved Jordan, too.

She knew it was true.

"We both miss you," she murmured, setting the photo down next to the one Tony had taken at the hospital. She had come to love the exhaustion in her face and the triumph there. She didn't look anything like the defeated woman who had been afraid she could not raise a child on her own. She looked strong and peaceful and joyous.

It had taken a while, but she finally felt that way, too.

Her path had led her through dark tunnels, but God had proved that there was always light waiting on the other side.

She hoped she would remember that when the next heartache happened.

And, it would.

There were no guarantees in life.

She understood that. Just like she understood that there would always be another celebration, another moment to enjoy, another reason to smile.

She was learning to be present in the moment, to enjoy each day and to embrace the miraculous moments in the midst of the ordinary. The sunrises and sunsets. The snow-laden branches of the towering evergreens. The first sweet call of the songbirds in spring.

The soft cooing of a baby waking to greet the day.

She glanced at the baby monitor and smiled as Jordyn Rose made herself known.

"Here I come, sweet girl," she said, hurrying to the nursery and lifting her from the crib.

Katie had already showered and dressed. She had read her Bible and had her quiet time. All she needed to do was change Jordyn Rose, feed her and grab the already-packed diaper bag, and she would be ready to ride to the graduation ceremony with Ivy and Alexander.

At 9:00 a.m. sharp.

Alexander had called her the previous evening to be sure she remembered. This would be Carter's last official day on the force, and Noah planned to give him an award for exemplary service.

She glanced at the clock.

Quarter past eight.

Forty-five minutes to feed and change the baby.

"Easy as pie," Katie said as she settled into the old rocking chair with her daughter.

Jordyn Rose still had chubby cheeks and a rosebud mouth. Her eyes had turned the same dark blue as Katie's, but her hair color had deepened. It was a rich chocolate brown, the fine thatch of hair she had been born with already growing into a shaggy mop of wild curls.

She was a beautiful baby, but it was her happy-go-lucky personality that always made Katie smile.

"You are a lot like your father, you know that?" she said, as Jordyn Rose sighed contentedly, milk dribbling from her mouth.

Katie should have known better than to get ready

before she fed the baby. She was learning quickly that messes happen, and they happen more when you have an infant.

"I am going to be a royal wreck before we even leave the house," she said, glancing at the clock.

"Come on, sweetheart. You need to eat up. We are going to see the puppies today. Grammy and Poppop are coming with us, and your uncles and Tony will be there. Come on. Let's get you burped. We still have plenty of time."

But, of course, when she had said that, she had not been counting on spit-up, or another diaper change.

She also had not counted on a lost baby shoe or a missing pacifier. By the time she finally managed to get them both dressed to semidecent standards, someone was knocking on the door.

"Hold on," she called breathlessly as she balanced Jordyn Rose in one arm and scooped the diaper bag off the floor.

She managed to open the door and nearly stumbled into her father-in-law, who was waiting on the landing.

"Whoa there, kiddo. We don't want to start the day with a wild ride down the stairs." He smiled as he steadied her, his eyes so much like Jordan's, she couldn't help smiling in return.

"It has been a bit of a rocky start to the day."

"Well, it is about to get a whole lot better. Hand me the bag and the kid, and let's get this show on the road."

"I can carry—"

"Are you going to deny me the pleasure of helping my favorite upstairs neighbor?"

"When you put it that way, I guess not," she said, laughing as she handed him the bag and the baby.

"You look lovely, Katie. Make sure you tell my wife I told you so."

"Did she put you up to it?"

"No. She simply commented that every man in her life knows how to give out a compliment. Except me. Apparently, she was the one who taught the skill to our sons and to Tony."

"They are all very good at it."

"Because they are all very good men. It is a nice thing to get to my age, look at your children, and know the values you tried to model and instill made a difference in their lives. I only wish…" He shook his head and headed down the stairs.

"That Jordan were here?" she guessed, knowing this day was as hard on the Jamesons as it was on her.

"What else would I want? I have a wonderful wife, great sons, beautiful young women who love them. I have two darling granddaughters. Life is good, but I will never stop missing Jordan."

"Until we see him again," she said quietly.

He glanced over his shoulder and offered a sad smile. "Until then."

"Are you two going to lollygag all morning?" Ivy called through the open window of the couple's Cadillac. "You know how bad traffic can be. If we don't get moving, we'll be late."

"Then we'd better hurry," Alexander said with a laugh as he opened the back door and put Jordyn in the car seat. Minutes later, they were on the way, weaving through morning traffic as they made their way to the canine-training center. It wasn't far, but traffic made it a long ride. By the time they arrived, the ceremony was almost ready to begin.

"We had better hurry," Ivy said, grabbing the diaper bag from the trunk. "It will be awkward if the chief's family walks in late."

They hurried across the parking lot, entered the auditorium and took their seats near the front. It didn't take long for the ceremony to begin. Noah gave a speech that honored Jordan and the legacy he had left behind—a strong K-9 Command Unit devoted to the community and to justice. In honor of his memory, a German shepherd puppy that had been deemed suitable for training was being named Jordy in keeping with the tradition of naming police dogs after fallen officers.

Surprised and touched, Katie wiped tears from her eyes as Noah put a collar bearing the name Jordy around the rambunctious dog's neck.

"Jordan would approve, don't you think?" Tony said, sliding into the seat beside her.

"I thought you were behind the stage with the graduates?" she whispered, leaning her head against his shoulder, loving the feel of his warmth against her cheek.

"I was relieved of my duty. Apparently, there has been a sudden change in the program. Noah asked all the K-9 officers to sit in the audience during this part."

"A sudden change?"

The last time the program had changed, it had been

because Jordan hadn't shown up. Two days later, his body had been found.

She shuddered, pulled her jacket a little closer and hugged Jordyn Rose a little tighter. She had every reason to be thankful for the life she had and for the second chances God had granted her. The day Martin's body had been recovered from the river, she had known she could move forward without fear, but sometimes she still felt haunted by the memories of all that had happened.

"A change doesn't have to be a negative thing," Tony reminded her.

"I know. It's just…"

"A lot of bad memories." He squeezed her hand, winding his fingers through hers and smiling as Jordyn Rose cooed.

"Hey, sweetheart," he whispered. "Want to sit with me?" He lifted Jordyn Rose gently, settling her into the crook of his arm.

Seeing them together filled Katie's heart in a way she never would have imagined could be possible. Even after heartache, love could grow. She knew that now. Understood just how surely God had been guiding her path through the tragedy of losing Jordan and the terror of being stalked by Martin.

Tony must have sensed her gaze.

He met her eyes and smiled, that simple sweet gesture filling her heart to overflowing.

"I love you," he mouthed.

"I love you, too," she responded and felt the joy of that to the depth of her soul.

When Noah finally placed the last K-9 police collar on the last graduating candidate, the crowd erupted with applause. The well-trained dogs stood near their handlers, tails wagging, tongues out. They would be put to good use in the community—searching for the missing, sniffing out explosives, finding drugs and offering closure to families by locating bodies of those long missing. There were German shepherds, Malinois, Labs and retrievers. A basset hound bayed happily as he trotted across the stage.

Jordyn Rose was wide-eyed and alert, her dark blue eyes focused on the dogs.

"I think you have a budding K-9 handler there," Alexander whispered as the last graduate crossed the stage.

"Maybe," she responded.

If that was the path God guided her daughter to, she wouldn't try to stop it.

*Go wherever He leads.*

That was what Jordan had always said, and that was what Katie planned to tell Jordyn Rose when she was old enough to understand.

Noah approached the podium again, with an unfamiliar young man beside him.

"Ladies and gentlemen and fellow dog lovers, as many of you know, our precinct has had a season of mourning. We lost Chief Jordan Jameson in a senseless act of violence. The day he was murdered, his K-9 partner, Snapper, disappeared. We spent countless hours searching for him. There were several possible sightings, but we were never able to verify them. Not long ago, one of our officers saw Snapper on the adoption website of a local shelter, but by the time we contacted them, and despite the fact that Snapper was microchipped, he had already been adopted out. Since then, we have made several attempts to contact his current owner, but we were unable to reach him. I'm going to be honest, I had just about given up hope of finding my brother's dog."

Noah stopped and took several deep breaths, obviously trying to control his emotion. "Two days ago, I received a call from Mr. Charles Williams. He has been on an in-field study trip with New York University. Charles is working on his PhD in botany. He was studying the flora of the Grand Canyon and just recently returned home. Before he left, he went to the local shelter and adopted a canine friend to bring along. Charles, can you bring him out for us?"

The young man walked backstage and reappeared a moment later with a beautiful German shepherd.

"Snapper!" Katie cried, jumping to her feet.

The dog's ears twitched, and he sniffed the air, and then, as if he finally understood he was home, he broke rank, jumping from the stage and barreling toward her.

She stepped out into the aisle to meet him, kneeling down to accept his doggy kisses. She didn't realize she was crying until Snapper nudged her cheek and pawed her shoulder.

"I am so happy you're back," she said as she looked into his dark, intelligent eyes.

"He looks great," Carter said, kneeling beside her and scratching Snapper's head. Zach joined them, running his hands down the dog's flanks and shaking his head.

"You wouldn't know he had ever been away from training."

"I know everyone is excited," Noah said above the din of the crowd's surprise. "But, if you could all settle down for a few moments, Charles has something he wants to say."

The young man stepped up to the podium, clearing his throat and adjusting the collar of his white dress shirt. He looked around the room, and his gaze found and settled on Katie.

"I had no idea of any of this when I adopted Roosevelt. Sorry, I mean Snapper. I named him Roosevelt after Theodore Roosevelt, but you don't need to know that."

The crowd laughed, and the young man continued, his gaze still focused on Katie. "What I *would* like you to know is that I had no idea Snapper was microchipped or that he was missing from the NYC K-9 Command Unit. I didn't know that his handler had been killed or that he had a family who missed him. I would also like you to know this—Snapper is everything a service dog should be. He's obedient, smart and driven. He is also loyal. He was always a good boy, but from the day I brought him home until the day I learned who he really was, I had the feeling that my buddy had better things to do with his time than lie around in the shade while I collected plant samples. So, as much as it pains me to do this, I've brought Snapper back home to you today. I hope he will have many more years of service to the community. Mrs. Jameson, please accept my deepest condolences for the death of your husband and my heartfelt thanks for sharing Chief Jameson's K-9 partner with me for these past weeks. I'm going to miss you, buddy," he said, not even trying to hide his tears.

Katie was crying again, and she didn't think there were many dry eyes in the audience. This was a beautiful end to a heart-wrenching story, and she was unbelievably grateful for it.

Noah concluded the ceremony by giving Carter an award for outstanding public service. The audience gave him a standing ovation as he walked stiffly from the stage. All these months later, he still had pain from the gunshot wound he had received in the line of duty, but soon he would be taking over the running of Griffin's Diner full-time. With his fiancée, Rachelle, by his side, and his daughter, Ellie, cheering him on, Katie had the feeling he would be just fine.

"You look happy," Tony whispered, his lips brushing her ear.

She shivered, turning so that they were looking into each other's eyes. "I have a lot to be thankful for."

"I think we all do," he said.

"Katie!" Ivy cried, throwing an arm around her shoulders. "What a blessing that Snapper is back." She crouched to pet the German shepherd, and he seemed to sigh contentedly.

"It really is."

"I guess he can retire now," Alexander said, taking Jordyn Rose from Tony's arms and tickling her under her chin.

She giggled and Snapper got to his feet, padding over to sniff her feet.

"See this little one?" Alexander knelt in front of Snapper. "She's Jordan's baby. What do you think of that?"

The baby and dog stared at each other.

Snapper nuzzled Jordyn Rose's cheek, huffed against her belly and then settled down again.

"He really is a great dog," Tony said. "Jordan always said he was the best German shepherd he had ever worked with."

"He did." Noah joined them, his fiancée, Lani, by his side.

"He *is* only five," Katie said, remembering all of the time Jordan and Snapper had spent training together. Hours and hours of work for what should have been eight to ten years of service.

"He'll have a good home with you," Noah said, but there was something in his voice that let her know he had been thinking what she had: Snapper was too young and too good to retire.

"Or, he can be assigned a new partner until he is old enough to retire, and then we can decide where he should live when he is an old man." Katie scratched Snapper's snout, and his tail thumped rhythmically.

"I think that's a great idea," Reed said, joining the small crowd of K-9 handlers, his wife, Abigail, and her emotional-support dog, Jet, beside him.

"Who do you think could handle him?" Luke Hathaway asked, his arm slung around his new wife, Sophie.

"If you want my opinion," Finn Gallagher said, "Lani is the perfect choice."

"Me?" Lani looked shocked, her eyes wide as she studied the faces of the other members of the K-9 team. Her time on the team had been limited, but she would always be part of the family they had become. If not for her relationship with Noah, she would have continued to be part of the team. They all knew and accepted that.

"I think it's a great idea," Finn's wife, Eva, said, her guide dog, Cocoa, beside her. "Not that I know much, but Finn keeps telling me what a great asset you were to the team. And, since you'll be working for another K-9 unit soon, why not be paired with Snapper?"

Soon the entire team was discussing the idea of Lani working with Snapper. Only Noah remained quiet. He probably felt that his relationship with Lani would make his opinion seem biased.

"I think," Tony interrupted, "Katie should make the decision. She has spent more time with Snapper than any of us."

The group went silent, all eyes fixed on Katie.

She looked at each of the men and women who had known and loved Jordan, and she thought about how much he had loved all of them. This was what he would want—the dog he had worked with so diligently being passed on to a fledgling handler. Both of them working together to serve the community he had loved.

"I think Lani and Snapper will make a good team," she said, her throat suddenly tight, her eyes burning.

Making the decision felt like turning the last page of a wonderful story—beautiful and sad, all at the same time.

"Are you sure?" Lani asked. "It's obvious he is

bonded with you, and I don't want you to feel like you have to allow him to keep working."

"It's what Jordan would want. It is what I want. So, yes, I'm sure. And, I do like that he'll stay in the family."

"I can't tell you how much this means to me," Lani said, pulling her in for a long hug.

"You know what would mean a lot to me?" Gavin Sutherland asked. "Going into the reception area and eating something. I don't know about everyone else, but I'm starving."

The group began walking away, but Katie stayed where she was, watching them leave, listening to their laughter. Near the doorway to the reception area, Ivy and Alexander were entertaining Ellie and Jordyn Rose. Noah and Lani were walking hand in hand, with their heads bent together. Carter and Rachelle were standing face-to-face, talking quietly as they looked into each other's eyes. Zach and Violet were just a few feet away, laughing quietly about something.

Katie couldn't help thinking that despite how their lives had been devastated, they had all found their joy again.

"What are you thinking?" Tony asked, his hands settling on her waist as he turned her so they were facing each other.

"Life. About how one season can bring sorrow and another joy. About family and how happy I am to be part of this one. Maybe even about love and how nice it is to see so many people find it."

"You know what I've been thinking?" He kissed her gently, his lips barely dancing across hers.

"That they probably have chocolate cake at the reception, and that's your favorite?"

He chuckled. "No. I've been thinking about life, too. About how one season brings loss and another abundance. About family and how much it means to be part of one. About love and how easy the word is to say when I'm with you. And, I've been thinking about forever and how wonderful it would be to spend it with you."

"Tony," she began, but she wasn't sure what she wanted to say. She didn't know if she could say anything that would be as beautiful as the words he had just spoken to her.

"I know this is a tough day, Katie. For all of us. And, I know that nothing can change that, but one thing I learned from losing Jordan is that now is never too soon to say what needs to be said."

He reached into his pocket, and her heart stopped. Her breath caught. The world seemed to stand still. He pulled out a small velvet box, and his hand shook just a little as he opened it.

"I never knew what home was until I met you. I never understood what it meant to belong until I looked into your eyes. I don't think I ever felt love until I sat in the hospital room with you and watched you hold your newborn daughter. I can't imagine walking through life without you by my side, and I can't imagine growing old with anyone but you. I love you, Katie. Will you marry me?"

She wanted to say yes. She did. But, the word stuck in her throat as tears flooded her eyes.

She reached for Tony, felt his arms close around her.

"It's okay to cry," he whispered against her ear. "It's okay to mourn what you lost."

"I know," she said, burying her face in the warmth of his chest. "But, I don't want to cry for what I've lost. I want to rejoice in what I have."

She stepped back, wiping tears from her eyes.

"When I lost Jordan, I closed myself off to love. I convinced myself that I would never meet someone who could melt the ice around my heart. I wasn't looking for love, Tony. I didn't even want it with you."

"Is that a yes?" someone asked, and she realized that the team had returned and was surrounding them, a wall of love created by people who knew the weight of Katie's sorrow and the depth of her loss. She didn't see judgment in any of their eyes; she saw joy.

"Yes, it is," she replied, levering up on her toes and kissing Tony with all of the passion and love she had to offer.

This second chance at happiness was a precious gift, and she wouldn't squander it. She wouldn't forget how miraculous each breath was, how beautiful each moment.

His arms slipped around her, and he pulled her close, his warmth reminding her of every bright sunrise after every long, dark night.

"Congratulations!" More than a dozen voices shouted in unison, the loudness of it scaring Jordyn Rose. She let out a high-pitched cry.

Katie pulled back, still looking into Tony's dark eyes as she took the baby from Alexander's arms. "I love you, Tony. Don't ever forget it."

He smiled, his lips skimming her forehead as he wiped a few tears from Jordyn Rose's face. When he finished, he lifted Katie's left hand and slid the ring on her finger.

She lifted her hand, surprised by the simple beauty of the stunning diamond solitaire, a small pink diamond nestled beside it. "It's beautiful, Tony."

"A diamond for each of my girls," he responded, lifting Jordyn Rose from Katie's arms and then taking her hand.

"Ready?" he asked, and she smiled.

"To eat?"

"To step into the future together."

"You know what?" she responded, pulling him a step closer. "I am."

\* \* \* \* \*

*If you enjoyed this series,*
*look for* True Blue K-9 Unit Christmas
*by Laura Scott and Maggie K. Black.*

Dear Reader,

Life is full of surprises. Some of them pleasant. Some not. In the book of Ecclesiastes, we are told that there is a season for everything under Heaven. A time to be born. A time to die. A time to rejoice. A time to mourn. Through the seasons of life, it is easy to get caught up in the sorrows rather than focusing on the joys. In the first seven books in the True Blue K-9 Unit series, you met heroes and heroines who have been through tough times and who have fought their way through doubts, disappointments and heartaches. With their trusty K-9 partners by their sides, they have sought answers to the murder of their beloved police chief, Jordan Jameson. Despite the challenges they face, they are able to cling to faith and trust in God to see them through.

Their stories resonate deeply with me. As someone who has faced very difficult seasons in life, I understand how easy it is to question God and His goodness, to wonder if He really cares. When we are deep in the darkest parts of our heartache, it can be difficult to see the light. But, even then, He is there. Whatever your challenges, remember—you are not alone.

And, because of that, you have the strength and courage to make it through to better times.

I love to connect with readers. Find me on Facebook, Twitter or Instagram, or drop me a line at shirleermccoy@hotmail.com.

Blessings,
*Shirlee McCoy*

# Get 4 FREE REWARDS!

## We'll send you 2 FREE Books plus 2 FREE Mystery Gifts.

**Love Inspired® Suspense** books feature Christian characters facing challenges to their faith... and lives.

**FREE** Value Over **$20**

SPECIAL EXCERPT FROM

*Love Inspired*
SUSPENSE

*When a police detective stumbles upon a murder scene
with no body, can the secret father of her child help her
solve the case without becoming the next victim?*

*Read on for a sneak preview of*
Holiday Homecoming Secrets *by Lynette Eason,
available December 2019 from Love Inspired Suspense.*

Bryce Kingsley bolted toward the opening of the deserted
mill and stepped inside, keeping one hand on the weapon
at his side. "Jade?"

"Back here." Her voice reached him, sounding weak,
shaky.

He hurried to her, keeping an eye on the surrounding
area. Bryce rounded the end of the spindle row to see
Jade on the floor, holding her head. Blood smeared a short
path down her cheek. "You're hurt!" For a moment, she
simply stared up at him, complete shock written across
her features. "Jade? Hello?"

She blinked. "Bryce?"

"Hi." He glanced over his shoulder, then swung the
beam of the flashlight over the rest of the interior.

"You're here?"

"Yeah. This wasn't exactly the way I wanted to let you
know I was coming home, but—"

"What are you doing here?"

"Can we discuss that later? Let's focus on you and the
fact you're bleeding from a head wound."

"I…I'm all right."

"Did you get a look at who hit you?"

"No."

A car door slammed. Blue lights whirled through the broken windows and bounced off the concrete-and-brick walls. Bryce helped her to her feet. "Let's get that head looked at."

"Wait." He could see her pulling herself together, the shock of his appearance fading. "I need to take a look at something."

He frowned. "Okay." She went to the old trunk next to the wall. "What is it?"

"The person who hit me was very interested in whatever was over here."

Bryce nodded to the shovel and disturbed dirt in front of the trunk. "Looks like he was trying to dig something up."

"What does this look like to you?"

"Looks like someone's been digging."

"Yes, but why? What could they possibly be looking for out here?"

"Who knows?" Bryce studied the pile of dirt and the bricks. "Actually, I don't think they were looking for anything. I think they were in the middle of *burying* something."

*Don't miss*
Holiday Homecoming Secrets *by Lynette Eason,*
*available December 2019 wherever*
Love Inspired® Suspense books and ebooks are sold.

LoveInspired.com

Looking for inspiration in tales
of hope, faith and heartfelt romance?

Check out **Love Inspired®** and
**Love Inspired® Suspense** books!

**New books available every month!**

---

**CONNECT WITH US AT:**

Facebook.com/groups/HarlequinConnection

Facebook.com/HarlequinBooks

Twitter.com/HarlequinBooks

Instagram.com/HarlequinBooks

Pinterest.com/HarlequinBooks

ReaderService.com

*Love Inspired®*

LIGENRE2018R2